Bailey wants to make her cousin Hannah feel welcome, but what do you do when your new friend copies everything you do?

Olivia stepped next to Bailey. "Do you feel like you're playing Simon Says? I mean Bailey Says?" Olivia said into Bailey's ear.

"What do you mean?" Bailey asked, half her attention on the volleyball game.

"It feels like Hannah's imitating you sometimes, what you wear, what you think is funny," Olivia explained. "Who you're friends with. Like tonight, she's been hanging with Gus almost the whole time. Doesn't it kind of bother you?"

PICTURE PERFECT

BETWEEN US

Cari Simmons and

Melinda Metz

HARPER

An Imprint of HarperCollinsPublishers

CHAPTER 1

How to Have an Epic First Week of Middle School

* * *

Prep

1. Go to mall with Olivia and check out what seventh and eighth graders are wearing. Then shop!
2. Start getting up at time you need to get up for school. No oversleeping. (Walking in late—yikes.)
3. Practice on combination lock.
4. Study map of school.
5. Organize school supplies.
6. Buy mints for locker.

When School Starts

1. Eat breakfast so stomach won't grumble.
2. Meet one person you didn't go to elementary school with.

3. Smile at people (but not like an insane clown girl).
4. Write down assignments.
5. Find out about clubs.
6. Remind Oh to use a straw so she won't spill!
7. Relax!!!!!

"I'm not sure you get to check off number seven," Olivia told her best friend.

"Why?" Bailey protested. Her fingers were itching to check off the last item on her Epic First Week list.

"How relaxed can you be if you have to have a list that tells you to be relaxed?" Olivia asked.

"Have you forgotten who you're talking to?" Bailey exclaimed, her voice rising. "Lists make me more relaxed than anything."

Olivia shook her head, setting her dark brown curls bouncing. "I just wanted to see how unrelaxed you'd get if you thought you'd have to leave something unchecked. You should have heard yourself squeak. It was like a mouse on helium."

"You're bad," Bailey told her, trying not to laugh. "A bad, bad friend." Bailey made an extrabig check next to number seven.

"Just trying to help you impulsify a little. You might

miss something good if you're always looking at a list," Olivia told her.

Bailey and Olivia were so different. Oh didn't like to plan. She didn't even like basic rules, such as using words that were actually in the dictionary.

"I can impulsify!" Bailey looked around, trying to think of a way to prove it. "Look! I'm . . . I'm *sing*-ing in pub-*lic*." She warbled the last few words, and didn't care that a couple of people turned around and stared at her.

Olivia gave a laugh that turned into a snort. "I can't believe you did that. I was horrifyingly close to spraying blueberry soda out of my nose."

"It would have been your own fault," Bailey teased. She took a sip of her raspberry drink. She and Olivia always went to Emmy's for Italian sodas when they had something to celebrate, and completing their first week of middle school was definitely what Olivia would call whoop-whoop worthy.

As different as they were, the two of them had been friends since the second grade. Somehow Bailey's love of planning and Olivia's willingness to try anything were a perfect combination. No matter how much time they spent together, they always wanted to be together more.

Bailey could probably fill a whole notebook with all the ways Olivia was an awesome friend. Her birthday was coming up in about a month. Maybe Bailey would make that list as part of her present. Olivia couldn't have a problem with a list like that!

"So next week at school, we should—" Bailey was interrupted by her cell clucking. She'd let Olivia set the ringtones. She checked it.

need you home. big news!

Bailey showed the text to Olivia. "I wonder what's up," Olivia said.

"Could be anything," Bailey answered. "Remember that text that said I had to get home ASAP, and it was because the first rosebud of the year was opening on one of her bushes?"

"That was cool. I love your mom," Olivia told her.

"Do you want to come with me?" Bailey asked. "Oh, wait. You can't. You've got karate." Olivia kept trying new sports to see if there was one where her klutziness wasn't a problem. Last year she'd taken dance. Kind of a disaster.

Olivia jumped up so fast she almost tipped over her chair. "I've got karate! I forgot!"

Bailey checked the time on her phone. "You're good. You have twenty-four minutes."

4

"Text me and tell me what the big news is," Olivia said as Bailey slid her notebook into her backpack.

"I will," Bailey promised.

"I'm home!" Bailey called as she opened the front door. She loved living so close to downtown, the whole street and a half of it. She could walk from Main Street to home in less than ten minutes. "So what's up?"

"Come sit with me in the kitchen," her mother called back.

Bailey's stomach clenched a little. Her mom sounded sort of upset. This didn't seem like it was going to be happy news, like the first rose of the season. She hurried into the kitchen and sat down.

"Are you hungry?" her mom asked.

Her mother didn't usually bother asking that. It's not as if Bailey didn't know where the hummus and veggies, her favorite after-school snack, were. Was she stalling? Bailey's stomach got a little tighter.

Bailey shook her head. "I had a piece of lemon cake at Emmy's." When her mother didn't say anything for a few seconds, Bailey added, "I got your text."

"Right. Right." Her mom straightened the napkins in the wooden holder. They were already perfectly straight.

Bailey was starting to wish she hadn't had the cake and soda. It didn't feel as if there was room for them in her stomach anymore. "Mom, please tell me what's going on."

Her mother must have heard the worry in Bailey's voice, because she smiled, crinkles appearing at the corners of her green eyes, the same green as Bailey's own. "It's nothing bad. Well, not bad for us." She pulled in a breath. "Your aunt Caitlin and your cousin Hannah are moving to Concord. They're going to be staying with your grandparents until they find a place of their own."

Bailey zoomed in on the important thing her mother hadn't said. "Just Aunt Caitlin and Hannah? Not Uncle Ethan?"

Her mother let out a long sigh. "They've decided to divorce," she explained. "They've been talking about it for a while. Now that the decision's made, Caitlin wants—well, a little cooling-down time. She doesn't know if she wants to live here in North Carolina permanently, but she wants to come for a bit. At least for the school year. She doesn't want Hannah to have to change schools twice in one year. She's had to change so many times already, with all the moving your uncle Ethan does in the military."

"I'd hate that," Bailey admitted. Starting middle school had made her a little nervous and a lot excited. But changing schools all the time? With all new people at every school? "Horrible" was the only word for it.

Her mother nodded. "Just starting at a new school in a new town is going to be hard enough, especially with her parents splitting up. And it's all happening so fast. Aunt Caitlin and Hannah will be here next Saturday."

"Wow." Bailey thought that having her parents living in different states would feel like the world getting pulled out from under her feet. Especially if she had to handle it without Olivia nearby. "Poor Hannah."

"You'll help her out, won't you?" her mother asked. "You have so many friends, and you know all the fun stuff to do in town. Even though Hannah's had to change schools a lot, her mom said she still finds it sort of scary."

"Definitely," Bailey answered. "I don't know everyone at school anymore, though. There are kids from other elementary schools, and some of my friends from Northeast Elementary are at different places." It had been strange to walk into classes this week and not recognize all the faces.

"You'll still have lots of people to introduce Hannah to. It's so great the two of you are in the same grade," her mother said. "I gave Aunt Caitlin your schedule. She's going to talk to the principal and see if she can get Hannah into some of the same classes."

"Cool," Bailey answered. "I'm trying to remember when the last time I even saw Hannah was."

"I was just thinking about that," her mother replied. "She and her parents came here for Christmas when you were both toddlers. The next time we saw them was four years ago, that time we went to Texas when your uncle was stationed at Fort Bliss."

My uncle who isn't going to be my uncle anymore, Bailey thought. *That's so weird.*

"I kind of remember. That's where they had that huge lizard in a cage at the gas station. It looked like it was covered with red and orange beads," Bailey asked.

"The Gila monster? That's what you remember?" Her mother laughed. "Yes, that was the place. Don't you remember Hannah at all?"

"I remember playing minigolf with her," Bailey answered.

"Right. *I'd* almost forgotten that part!" her mother exclaimed. "You both somehow decided it was a lot more fun to hit the balls into the water than into the holes."

That brought the day back a little more clearly. She remembered being mad because Hannah had grabbed the red ball after Bailey had called it. But they'd had fun splashing around in the fountains to retrieve their balls whenever they "accidentally" whacked them into the water.

Her mother's cell rang. She glanced at it. "That's your aunt again. I can tell her that you'll help Hannah fit in and introduce her to everybody, right? It will make both of them feel better."

"I promise," Bailey said. Her mother smiled at her as she picked up the phone.

Bailey headed to her bedroom. There were no phones allowed in the dojo where Olivia took karate lessons, but there was enough time to text her before she had to go in.

my cousin's moving here. going to r school.

??? Olivia texted back.

No wonder Olivia didn't know who she was talking about. Hannah was Bailey's cousin and Bailey had seen her only once—well, once that she remembered. Bailey typed in a response.

hannah. our grade. all i know.

here 4ever? Olivia texted.

not sure. parents getting divorce.

sad, Olivia texted.

mom wants me 2 be her friend. so you have 2 2.

kk. if she's cool, Olivia answered.

She added a jk before Bailey could answer.

she's my cuz, Bailey texted. gotta b cool. ;)

CHAPTER 2

How to Make Hannah Feel Incredibly Welcome

1. Give her a tour of school.
2. Take her to S&I Ice Cream.
3. Introduce her to Olivia, Vivi, and Tess.
4. Make fruit star cookies for lunch when she gets here.
5. Invite her to sit with you at lunch in caf.
6. Decorate her locker.
7. Invite her to walk to school with you and Olivia.
8. Program your number into her cell.
9. Take her to Kitty City to visit the kittens.
10. Get her notes for the days she's missed in all her classes.
11. Go to Pickin & Grinnin and find a fun welcome present.
12. Help Grandma get the guest room ready.
13. Take her to the big mall—including the aquarium!

Bailey put the snow globe in the middle of the dresser and gave a nod of satisfaction. It was the perfect welcome present. Inside was a cute black-and-white cow riding a Ferris wheel. Little stars flew around when you shook it. WELCOME TO THE CABARRUS COUNTY FAIR was printed on the base. Bailey had known she'd found exactly the right thing when she'd seen that the globe actually said "welcome" on it. Maybe next summer Hannah would be able to go to the fair, if she was still living here.

"Pickin and Grinnin?" Grandma asked as she ran her fingers lightly over the globe.

"Of course," Bailey answered. She and her grandmother both loved the little thrift store.

"She'll adore it," her grandmother said. "I'm so glad Hannah has you in town to help her get settled."

"And Olivia," Bailey reminded her.

"Of course, Olivia," Grandma said. "That goes without saying. Where there's Bailey, there's Olivia. And where there's Olivia, there's Bailey." She looked around the room. "Is there anything I've forgotten?"

Bailey checked the list she'd made on Bedroom Basic Necessities. She opened the closet. "Hangers!" she announced.

"Right. I don't know what I'd do without you and those lists of yours. BRB." She hurried out of the room.

Bailey smiled. Her grandmother was doing great with the abbreviations. Bailey had made her a list of the most common ones when her grandmother had started playing bridge online. She sat down on the four-poster bed. Her bed. At least she'd always thought of it as hers. It was where she slept every time she stayed at her grandparents'.

She stretched out, smelling the familiar lavender scent of her grandmother's linen spray. Her eyes immediately found the crack in the ceiling that looked like a leaf. She wondered how many times she'd slept in this bed. Probably once a week since she was five. She loved having her grandparents right around the block.

She sat up again, suddenly realizing that with Hannah and Aunt Caitlin living with her grandparents, she wouldn't be able to have her usual nights staying over. The whole time she'd been helping get Hannah's room ready, it hadn't quite hit her that the room wouldn't be hers anymore.

But it's not as if Hannah could sleep on the sofa so Bailey's room would be free whenever she wanted it! That wouldn't make her feel very welcome. And the plan wasn't just to make her cousin feel welcome. The plan was to make Hannah feel *incredibly* welcome.

As soon as the last bell rang on Friday, Bailey headed for her cousin's locker. It was kind of amazing to her how at home she already felt at the middle school. Two weeks ago, she'd had to refer to her mental map whenever she went to class. Now she moved through the halls on autopilot.

"Hey, Oh!" she called when she turned the corner. Her best friend was already waiting for her. "How was the Spanish quiz?"

"*Muy bueno, gracias,*" she answered. "Except I forgot how to say 'banana.' And it's just '*banano*'! That's one letter different!"

"You must have had some kind of mental block," Bailey said. Olivia hated the way bananas squished when you bit into them. She called it "squicked."

Olivia shrugged. "I guess it doesn't matter that much. I'm not going to ever want to ask for one."

"Learn to say, 'Keep that yellow thing far, far away from me.' Just in case of a *banano*-related emergency," Bailey joked. She pulled out her cell and checked it. "Hannah texted me!" she exclaimed. She'd decided a few days ago that she should text Hannah to say she was excited about her moving to Concord. She hadn't thought of that when she'd made her list. After she had sent the first one, they'd texted back and forth a few more times.

"What did she say?" Olivia asked.

"She asked if people usually bring their lunch or buy it. That's it," Bailey answered. "She's had a lot of questions like that. The other day she wanted to know what electives I'm taking."

"I wonder if she's freaking out. I'd be freaking out. She has to be freaking out," Olivia said. "I mean, I was freaking out about starting here, and I know tons of people."

"Me too. But at least she'll have me and you and Vivi and Tess, for starters," Bailey replied.

"So all the best people," Olivia joked. "Here comes the office lady!"

Yesterday Bailey had asked if she could get the combination for Hannah's locker so she could decorate it. The office lady, Ms. Durban, had told her no. It was against the rules to give anyone but the student the combination. But Bailey had convinced her how important it was to make Hannah feel welcome, and she'd agreed to unlock the locker for them—just that one time.

"Don't peek," Ms. Durban said before she dialed in the combination, and Bailey and Olivia obediently closed their eyes. "All done," Ms. Durban announced a moment later. "This is very considerate of you girls.

Make sure you close the locker door when you're done," she added as she walked away.

"Time to bring the fabulous!" Olivia cried. She pulled a square of fluffy lavender carpet out of her backpack and spread it on the bottom of the locker.

Bailey used magnets to attach a rectangle of lavender-and-orange-striped wallpaper to the back wall. She'd cut it to size the night before. She'd wrecked a few sheets trying to get it right. She wasn't exactly what anyone would call crafty.

"I nabbed this from Rose's dress-up box." Olivia held out a white feather boa. "I thought it would make cool trim."

"Awesome! You rock! I just don't want to be around when Rose finds out it's missing." Olivia's little sister was known for truly epic tantrums.

"Me neither," Olivia said as they used more magnets to attach the boa around the inside of the locker door. "But if I am, it'll be worth it. Anything for your cousin."

"I'm here!"

"Me too!"

Bailey smiled as she saw Vivi and Tess rushing toward them. Tess had her skateboard in one hand. She'd be on it as soon as she hit the sidewalk.

"Mirror and pic," Vivi said. She handed the items

to Bailey, then smoothed a few flyaway hairs back into place in her sleek bob. Bailey had asked all three of her friends to bring pictures of themselves for Hannah's locker. She wanted Hannah to know she had some go-to girls if Bailey wasn't around.

"Perfection." Bailey added the mirror to the inside door and used a flower-shaped magnet to stick Vivi's picture up.

"I didn't forget my stuff for tweaking the locker," Tess said. "How could I, with a reminder text, IM, and phone message?"

Vivi and Olivia cracked up. "I know, I know, I micromanage," Bailey admitted.

Tess gave Bailey a small dry-erase board and a picture. "Let's all sign it before you put it up," Olivia suggested.

Vivi drew a cartoon of the four of them giving big waves. She could draw anything. Then they all signed under their cartoon selves.

"Anything missing?" Bailey asked when she'd put up all the pictures and stocked the locker's top shelf with mints, a bottled water, pens—because you could never have enough pens—a couple of hair ties, and a little bottle of hand lotion.

Her friends laughed again as she pulled a list out of

the front pocket of her backpack.

"You're asking us?" Olivia said. "I can just imagine your face if one of us actually came up with something that wasn't on your list." She stretched her lips into a grimace of horror and bugged out her eyes.

"Go ahead, mock me! But while you mock, look at how beautiful the locker turned out," Bailey said as she started going over her list one more time. When she finished, she looked up at her friends. "Do I make you totally crazy with my reminders and lists?" she asked. "It's just . . . when I know I've planned everything out, I don't have to stress that I've forgotten something important. I can just have fun!"

"Truth?" Tess asked.

Bailey nodded, bracing to hear how annoying she was.

"I actually did forget about bringing the locker stuff until I got your text," Vivi said. That got everyone laughing again. "It's just that last night I was visualizing myself doing a three-sixty nightmare flip. This blog I read says visualizing can help when you're working on a new trick. I got kind of distracted," she admitted.

"It's like we're the Avengers. We all have our superpower. Tess has skateboarding. Vivi has art. You have being organized, Bails. And I'm good at everything—except walking without tripping over all the invisible stuff lying around," Olivia joked. "We make a great team!"

"I think so too." Bailey used a tissue to wipe away a tiny smudge on the locker's mirror, then nodded. "I pronounce it Hannah-ready," she declared.

"I can't believe it! I forgot to find out if Hannah is a vegetarian or a vegan or eats gluten-free or anything like that," Bailey moaned. She'd just arranged the ingredients for baking cookies on the kitchen counter. "The cookies have eggs and flour. And the icing has cream cheese! What if Hannah is lactose intolerant?"

"I guess I'll just have to eat all the cookies myself," her dad joked. He sat at the kitchen table working the crossword puzzle in pen. He said doing the puzzle in pencil was for wimps.

"Maybe I should text her," Bailey said.

"Just go ahead and make them and don't worry about it," her mom told her. She was at the kitchen table too, having a second cup of coffee. "They'll be getting ready to head to the airport. Caitlin's probably frantic. They haven't had much time to pack and put things in storage and do everything else they needed to do."

"Okay, okay," Bailey muttered. She studied the

recipe, even though she almost had it memorized. The star-shaped cookies with thin strawberry slices on each arm of the star were her faves. There was a slice of kiwi in the middle, and the colors of the fruit made the cookies so pretty. She hoped Hannah liked them as much as she did.

She'd just finished mixing the batter when the kitchen door banged open and Gus came strolling in. He acted like he lived there, because he'd lived next door his entire life. Bailey's mom called him Bailey's "brother from another mother."

"Greetings, Broadwell family," Gus called out.

"Gus, what a nice surprise," Bailey's father teased. Gus came over every Saturday morning after he finished his paper route, for a second breakfast. He had his first before he headed out to deliver the papers.

"Isn't it?" Gus joked back. He opened a cupboard, pulled out the Cocoa Krispies, poured himself a bowl, and then added chocolate milk from the fridge. "Whatcha making?" he asked as he perched on the counter next to Bailey's mixing bowl.

"Fruit star cookies," she answered, blocking his spoon before he could send it diving into the batter.

"Make me some without the fruit," he said.

"The strawberries are fine. I could do without the

kiwi," her father commented.

"I'm not making them for either of you. They're for Hannah. And Aunt Caitlin," Bailey informed them.

Gus reached behind him and opened the cabinet with the spices. He pulled out a bottle of Satan's Rage Hot Sauce. The stuff was as red as Gus's hair. Bailey's dad loved it on his eggs. "You know what those cookies really need?" Gus pulled off the top. "Some of *this*!" He tilted the bottle over the bowl, and Bailey snatched it out of his reach with a squeal.

A lot of times Gus was fun to hang out with, but a lot of times he was incredibly annoying. Just like a real brother, at least according to Vivi. "Out!" Bailey ordered. "You are banished until this afternoon. At least. I'm making lunch. Cooking and Gus don't go together."

"What's the big deal? You make cookies all the time, and they're always pretty edible," Gus told her, not leaving.

"Hannah's going through a really hard time," Bailey explained. "I know having everything perfect for lunch can't change that. But maybe it will make her a little bit happier."

CHAPTER 3

How to Serve a Perfect Lunch

• • •

1. Schedule plenty of time to make food.
2. Create a playlist of background music.
3. Have a signature drink.
4. Set table early—make swan napkins!
5. Make sure flower arrangement is low enough to talk over.
6. Prepare conversation topics in case no one is talking.
7. Relax!!!!

The swan napkins didn't look swanlike. Or even birdlike. They looked like . . . Bailey stared at them. They looked like lumpy twists of cloth. This was so frustrating. She'd followed the instructions exactly!

She should start over, except everyone should be here pretty much now. It would be worse if they walked in and she had half the swans redone and half still lumps, wouldn't it? The decision was made for her when she heard a knock on the door.

"I'll get it!" Bailey exclaimed. She straightened her hostess apron. The blog she'd read said it was fine to greet guests in one, and she loved the one she'd found at the thrift store. It was brown with white polka dots, and it had a cute little pink bow on one side at the waist.

"Here they are!" her grandfather exclaimed when she threw open the door. He gestured to her aunt and cousin, with a huge grin on his face. Her grandmother was beaming too.

"How are you? How was the trip? Are you exhausted?" Bailey's mother asked in a rush as she flew over to Aunt Caitlin and gave her a long hug. "And look at you, Hannah," she continued, even though she hadn't gotten answers to any of her questions. "You're so grown-up." Her mom hugged Hannah too. When she let her go, she said, "This is your cousin, Bailey."

"Hi. I'm glad you're here," Bailey said, just the way she'd planned. She smiled at her cousin. She really barely remembered her. Hannah still wore her blond hair long, all the way down her back, but besides that, Bailey wasn't sure what was the same and what was different. Other than that she was bigger and older, of course.

"Hi," Hannah answered. That was all. Just hi. She looked a little dazed. Well, why wouldn't she?

"Who wants one of the signature cocktails for the day?" Bailey asked.

"Cocktail?" Her grandfather raised his eyebrows.

"Well, mocktail. It's watermelon lemonade," Bailey answered.

"Every occasion should have a signature drink. And your moving here is definitely an occasion," Bailey's mom told Aunt Caitlin and Hannah. Bailey nodded. Her mother got it. She understood that Bailey wanted her aunt and cousin to know that their moving to town deserved a celebration.

"Then watermelon lemonades all around," her grandmother said.

Bailey rushed to the kitchen. She had two pitchers of the lemonade in the fridge, and she'd put the glasses in the freezer about two hours ago to frost. She'd made ice cubes out of the lemonade too, so the drinks wouldn't get all watery when the cubes melted.

Her mom came in when Bailey was placing the glasses on a tray. "Oooh, frosted glasses. Classy!" she exclaimed. "Why don't you carry the tray, and I'll bring the pitcher?"

"Thanks," Bailey answered.

"You've done a beautiful job, sweetie," Mom said. "I'm so proud of how hard you've worked to make Hannah and Aunt Caitlin feel welcome."

A warm burst of happiness flooded Bailey. "It took a couple lists," she admitted.

"I bet." Her mother got one of the pitchers out of the fridge and led the way to the living room.

Bailey tried not to stare at Hannah when she took her first sip. But she really, really just wanted her to like it. "Do you like it?" she blurted out, almost before her cousin was able to swallow.

"It's really good," Hannah answered. She took another tiny sip.

"Hannah's not crazy about watermelon. Ever since—" Aunt Caitlin began.

"But it's different as a drink. It's really good!" Hannah interrupted, taking a gulp, a gulp that left her glass almost half-empty.

Bailey noticed that Hannah gave the tiniest of grimaces as she set the glass down. She really didn't like the mocktail, even though she was being super nice about it. Bailey should have made two signature drinks, so Hannah would have had a choice!

It was okay, though. Bailey had lots of other great stuff planned to make Hannah's first day in town extraspecial.

"So this is Main Street," Bailey told Hannah. She suddenly wondered if Concord might feel boring compared to all the places Hannah had lived. Her family had even lived in Brazil one year! "I know it's tiny, but it's not like everything in town is here. We have a mall pretty close by, and then a really big mall that only takes about fifteen minutes to drive to."

"It's really cute," Hannah answered. She sounded like she really meant it.

"I think so too," Bailey said. "So first up, we have the bead store. My friend Vivi, you'll meet her at school, is really into crafts. She goes in there a ton. Me, I'm not so crafty, as you might have been able to tell by the swan lumps I made out of the napkins."

Hannah laughed. "I'm not really that crafty either," she admitted. Although Bailey had seen her fold her napkin into a swan that looked exactly like the picture online, before she'd unfolded it again and put it in her lap. She'd done it automatically, like she wasn't even thinking about it.

"Then we have the chocolatier. Amazing chocolate. A-*maz*-ing. And across the street is Gianni's Pizza. They have the best pizza." Bailey hoped she didn't sound like she was bragging. "I hope I don't sound like I'm bragging," she told Hannah, deciding it was better to just say it. "I just want you to know you'll be living in a great place."

Hannah nodded, and for a second Bailey thought she saw tears in her cousin's green eyes, the same green as her own; but Hannah blinked, and if the tears had been there, they had disappeared. This had to be so hard for her.

Bailey promised herself she was going to try even harder than she'd planned to make Hannah happy here. "Kitty City!" she exclaimed, remembering number nine on her list of How to Make Hannah Feel Incredibly Welcome. She loved that place. And if you were feeling sad and homesick, what could make you feel happier faster than kittens? "It's this cat rescue place right down the block. I love to go in and visit. Want to go?"

"Sure," Hannah answered.

"Great! Last time there was this big old cat with seven toes on both front feet. Libby, one of the volunteers, told me cats with extra toes are called

Hemingway cats. He was so sweet. He had the loudest purr you've ever heard," Bailey said as they continued down the block. "Oh, good! They have kittens!" she exclaimed as they passed the huge glassed-in cat play areas on either side of the entrance.

Libby was working. "Can we take the new kittens out?" Bailey called.

"Of course," Libby answered. "You know we love to get them used to people." She coaxed the kittens out onto the floor. Bailey gently picked up one with the sweetest little face and handed him to Hannah. "Libby, this is my cousin Hannah. She just moved to town."

"Welcome," Libby said. "I hope you'll like it here."

"I'm sure I will," Hannah answered.

Bailey noticed Hannah was holding the kitten away from her body, carefully cupped in both hands. "You can cuddle him. It's okay." She pressed Hannah's hands closer to her body, so the kitten could snuggle against her. The kitten immediately began to knead Hannah's T-shirt with its tiny baby claws.

Bailey smiled. Hannah already had new friends— Libby and the kitten. She scooped up another kitten from the litter and giggled when it lightly licked her hand. Its tongue felt as rough as an emery board. "Aren't you the most adorable little thing?" she murmured. "Aren't you? Aren't you?"

Her cousin sneezed. Then sneezed again. Then gave three more sneezes, without even a second in between them. Bailey reached into her bag for a tissue. Her hand froze when she saw her cousin's face and neck. They were covered with red splotches.

"Uh-oh. You must be allergic," Libby said, taking the kitten away from Hannah.

"I am," Hannah admitted.

"Why didn't you tell me?" Bailey wailed. She put her kitten back on the floor and handed Hannah the tissue. "We shouldn't have come in here. It's practically made out of cat hair."

"I know, but I love kittens," Hannah said. She sneezed again. She looked completely miserable. "I think I should go home." Her face squinched up when she said "home." "Back to your house, I mean, and get some Benadryl."

Bailey hadn't gotten to show Hannah even half the things she'd wanted to. Her tour had turned into a complete disaster!

"Oh no!" Olivia cried when Bailey called her later that night and told her what had happened. "But why didn't she just tell you she was allergic?"

"I don't know," Bailey answered. "She said she loves kittens. Maybe she thought she could pet a couple of them without getting a reaction. But by the time we got home, her face was so puffy it was like her eyes had almost disappeared. It was awful."

"Poor Hannah. And poor you. I know you wanted her first day to be perfectabulous," Olivia said. "We'll make it up to her when we take her to the mall tomorrow. We're still going, right?"

"Yep. My mom and Aunt Caitlin are coming too, but they're going to go off by themselves. We can do what we want," Bailey answered. "We'll pick you up at one, 'kay?"

"Sounds good. Don't worry. We'll have so much fun, Hannah will forget her first day ended in sneezes and tears and blotches!" Olivia promised.

"What else can we tell you about school, Hannah?" Bailey asked.

"We're complete experts now that we've been there for two weeks!" Olivia joked, and Hannah laughed.

They stepped to the side as the mall's kiddie train moved slowly toward them. "I can't think of anything, since you're giving me a tour before school tomorrow. I'm sure I'll have questions once I'm there, though."

"How about questions about living in the South, Yankee?" Olivia teased.

Hannah raised her eyebrows. "Yankee?"

"Absolutely," Bailey answered. "Everybody who wasn't born and raised in the South is."

"Is that a thing? Will people not like me because I'm not from here?" Hannah sounded worried. "We lived in Texas for a little while. Does that count?"

"Not really. Like I said, born and raised. But don't stress. It's no big thing," Bailey reassured her. "I mean, somebody might joke around about it, but it's no big deal."

"A lot of places, people make fun of new people," Hannah said.

"Well, here you have us," Bailey told her.

"Right, with two friends, you can't really be new," Olivia assured her. "What can we tell her to make her feel more like a local?" she asked Bailey.

"Oh, here's something. You and your mom say CON-curd. It's Con-CHORD." Bailey emphasized the second syllable.

"And the mountains are App-a-LATCH-un and not App-a-LAY-shun," Olivia chimed in again. "Tourists always get that wrong. Not that you're a tourist. And Cheerwine is not a wine. I seriously heard someone order it in a restaurant like that once. It's cherry soda."

"The yummiest. Did they have it anywhere you've lived?" Bailey asked.

"Uh-uh." Hannah had started nibbling on her lip. She brightened. "But there were some strange sodas other places. Like in England, there was one called Dandelion and Burdock. It was really made with dandelions! And in Japan there's this version of Pepsi called Pepsi White. It has a sort of yogurty taste."

Olivia wrinkled her nose. "Yogurt Pepsi. Sounds nasty." She grinned. "I want to try one."

"My dad and I always tried all the sodas everywhere we went," Hannah said, some of the enthusiasm draining from her voice.

"You'll have to send him a Cheerwine! It's made right near here, in Salisbury," Bailey told her.

"I think it's so cool you've lived so many places," Olivia said.

"It is. But it takes a while to figure out everything," Hannah said. "By the time I'm starting to feel settled, *bam*, we're moving again."

Bailey noticed that her cousin had gotten a little pale. Her brows had pulled together, and she was biting her lip again. *Uh-oh.* "Don't worry. This won't be like the other places."

Olivia, being her best friend, got it. "Let's go get a Cheerwine right now. Then you'll know what it is. Easy-peasy."

"Right. To the food court!" Bailey exclaimed.

Ten minutes later, they'd grabbed a table by the carousel. They watched the little kids ride as they drank their sodas. "Bailey and I always rode the zebra and the sea horse. They're right next to each other."

"So you've known each other a long time?" Hannah asked.

"We've been besties since we were in the same second-grade class," Bailey answered.

"Wow. I haven't had any friends that long," Hannah said.

"The biggest trauma of my life was when Bailey and I got assigned to different teachers in fifth," Olivia added.

"Mine too! It was horrible!" Bailey agreed.

Hannah looked down and took a long, long sip of her drink.

Bailey suddenly realized how dumb she and Olivia had been. They called being split up in the fifth grade traumatic. And here was Hannah, whose parents were getting divorced and who was ultrastressed about living in another new place.

Subject change, Bailey decided. That's what was needed. "Did you already get your schedule?" she said to Hannah. "I can't believe I didn't ask you that before. We should see if we're in any classes together."

"Bails and I have English and math together," Olivia said. "And the same lunch."

Hannah pulled a piece of paper out of her bag and spread it on the table. "I printed it out from an email. They're giving me the regular copy tomorrow."

"We're in the same homeroom!" Bailey exclaimed. "Cool! And you're in math with me and Olivia. And we all have the same lunch."

"And the two of us are in history together," Olivia said. "Our friend Vivi is in that class. You'll like her. Oh, and I think Tess might be in your English class. I'm pretty sure she has it third period."

"We have science together too, and drama and track," Bailey added. "Wow, we chose the same electives. Think acting and running run in the family?" She laughed.

"My mom talked to the principal and got her to put me in the same electives as you," Hannah answered. "She tried to get me in all the same classes, since I'm new and everything, but it didn't work out. At least we have four, though." She smiled at Olivia. "And one with you."

"Your mom wanted you to be in *all* the same classes as Bailey?" Olivia asked. Bailey could tell Oh thought that was a little weird.

"I'm glad you got in so many of the same ones," Bailey told Hannah. It would be fun. She and Hannah could study together, and it would be even easier for Bailey to introduce Hannah to everyone with them being in the same classes.

"So where to next?" Olivia asked. She had finished her soda and was crunching on some of the ice.

"Where do you want to go, Hannah? Claire's? Bookstore? There's a fun arcade." Bailey threw out suggestions.

"Mmmm. I don't know," Hannah said. "Wherever you want."

"This is your first time at the mall. We want to go where you want to go," Olivia protested.

"I guess I just don't know what's here," Hannah answered.

Even though Bailey had just told her three things.

"They have pretty much everything," Bailey said. "What are you in the mood for? Shoes? Music? Frozen yogurt? There's a photo booth where you can make goofy pictures."

Hannah just gave a little shrug. Bailey gave Olivia a hopeless look.

"I know!" Olivia said. "We should shop for a scarf for Hannah. Or do you have a bunch already?"

"I have one I usually wear with my coat when it's cold," Hannah answered.

"You're going to need at least one more. Everybody at school, all the girls anyway, wears scarves. Bailey noticed when we did our pre-middle-school reconnaissance."

"What?" Hannah asked.

"Bailey came up with the idea to come here and watch what all the older kids were wearing, so we'd know what to wear the first day," Olivia explained. "In case you haven't noticed, Bailey is very organized. She has a plan for everything."

"That was a good idea," Hannah told Bailey.

Bailey grinned. "Thanks," she said. "It turns out it's partly because of the dress code. You're not supposed to wear shirts that go more than two and a half inches below your collarbone. So no V-necks. But if you wear a scarf that covers up that bare area, it's okay. Even when girls are wearing shirts that go high enough, a lot of them wear scarves anyway. It's a thing."

"It's so great to have someone to tell me this stuff. I never have before. There were kids at the bases, but I didn't get to know them right away, so I had to figure out everything by myself." Hannah answered. "Thanks so much."

"You're welcome," Bailey said. It felt good to help out her cousin.

"There's a kiosk that sells really cute ones," Olivia said. She looked over at Hannah. "Want us to show you?"

"Absolutely!" Hannah exclaimed. She sounded pretty cheerful again. Bailey's welcome plan must be working. *Yay!*

Olivia led the way to the kiosk. "I've got one kind of like this," she said, fingering an infinity scarf with a loose weave. The color shifted from pale blue to pale green and back. "I love how soft it is."

The teen girl working at the kiosk smiled at her. "I remember you. And your friend." She nodded at Bailey. "I have an excellent memory for customers. You bought . . ." She squeezed her eyes shut for a long moment, then opened them and pointed at a bright yellow scarf with turquoise polka dots.

"Right!" Bailey told her. "Polka dots are kind of

my thing." She gestured toward her sneakers. Their shoelaces had polka dots in a rainbow of colors. Then she waved her hands so the girl could see her polka-dotted nails.

"I'm a polka dot person too." Hannah held up her hand, so Bailey slapped her a high five. Then Hannah slowly circled the cart, looking at each scarf. "I'm going to get this one!" she announced.

The scarf was a mirror image of Bailey's—turquoise with bright yellow polka dots. Bailey grinned. She and Hannah both liked polka dots. It wasn't a huge thing, but it was a start. Maybe she and her cousin would end up being amazing friends.

CHAPTER 4

How to Do a Scene with a Weak Actor

• • •

1. Find something good in what they do—and praise them.
2. Take charge of what you do as a team.
3. Don't let their performance shake your confidence.
4. Respond to what your partner is doing.
5. Have fun with it.
6. Relax!!!

As Bailey walked toward the cafeteria Monday morning, she texted Hannah a reminder of where Bailey and her friends would be sitting. She and Hannah were in a bunch of classes together, but not the one right before lunch.

Hannah was already sitting with Olivia and Vivi when Bailey walked in. Bailey gave her a big smile and a wave, then got in the lunch line. She'd brown-bagged it, so all she had to do was grab a drink. She picked out an orange juice, paid, then hurried over to the table. "You met Vivi already. Great," she said.

"We were just in history together. Olivia too," Hannah said. "Thanks for putting the pictures in my locker. I recognized Vivi right away."

"You're welcome," Bailey answered. She could tell Hannah really appreciated it. And Hannah had been totally thrilled when she saw the way Bailey and the others had decorated her locker. It was so sweet how excited she'd gotten.

Bailey's eyes snagged on Hannah's fingers as Hannah raised her sandwich to her mouth. Hannah had done her nails in polka dots, in addition to wearing her new polka-dotted scarf. They really were soul sisters! Bailey painted polka dots on her nails. It was her signature look.

"It's so cute the way you did your nails!" she said. Hannah had painted the tips of her nails white with black dots, then she'd done a strip of deep rose with a tiny black bow glued on.

"I want those bows!" Vivi cried.

"I saw some online and I decided to try making them. I have a bunch. I'll bring them tomorrow, and you can all pick some," Hannah volunteered.

Bailey thought of something she wanted to ask. "Hannah, how did you like Mr. Moya? I have him too, right before your class. He cracks me up."

"Me too!" Hannah exclaimed. "He's so funny. Today he told this joke about the Americans licking the British because of the Stamp Act."

"He told us that too," Bailey said. "Insanely corny."

"Well, yeah, that one actually wasn't so good," Hannah answered quickly.

"Which is what made it so hilarious." Bailey pulled her sandwich out of her lunch bag.

"Right, so bad it was good!" Hannah spoke so quickly her words almost smashed into each other.

"This is Mr. Moya after one of his jokes," Vivi said. She held up a sketch she'd done on a napkin that showed the teacher laughing so hard he was crying.

"No matter what anyone else thinks, *he* loves his jokes," Olivia added.

"They had pizza. I'm stoked," Tess said as she set down her tray.

"School pizza doesn't even taste like pizza, though," Olivia complained.

"That's your problem. You expect it to taste like pizza. If you don't expect it to taste like pizza and just appreciate it on its own, it's yummy," Bailey said.

"So yummy," Hannah agreed.

"You haven't even tried it yet," Vivi said. "I'm with Olivia. It's gross."

Vivi was right. Hannah hadn't had their school pizza. How'd she know if it was good or not?

"It's just that it looks like the same pizza we had at a couple of my schools," Hannah explained. "That same thick crust that's almost like bread."

"Here, taste it and see if it's the same." Tess tore off a corner and passed it to Hannah.

Hannah took a little bite, then took a long swallow of her milk. "Even yummier than at the other schools," she pronounced. But Bailey noticed she didn't eat the rest of the little piece. She set it in the far corner of her tray.

Bailey's phone vibrated in her pocket. She pulled it out and saw that Olivia had sent her a text from across the table.

how does it feel having a clone?

w? Bailey texted back, holding the phone under the table.

yer cuz is dressed like you. sez she likes everything you like.

Bailey glanced over at Oh and shrugged. cause I'm fab! She texted back.

Olivia smiled. A second later, a new text from her showed up.

yep. even i want to be u. ;)

***

"We have a new student in our class," Ms. Healy announced that afternoon. "Hannah Sullivan." She gestured towards Hannah. "Why don't you tell us a little about yourself, Hannah?"

"Bailey Broadwell is my cousin." She gave Bailey a big smile, and Bailey smiled back. "What else? Um . . ." Hannah's eyes flicked back and forth, like she might see some interesting fact about herself written on one of the posters hanging on the walls.

"Hannah's lived all over, even in Brazil and Japan and England," Bailey chimed in.

"Cool," said a girl Bailey hadn't met yet.

Hannah looked relieved. "I'm looking forward to living here."

"It sounds like you'll have a lot of great experiences to draw on in your acting," Ms. Healy told Hannah. "All right, today we're going to do some exercises that will help you pay attention to the other actors you're working with. Listening is as important as saying lines. You need to be really aware of the other people in a scene with you. Everybody grab a partner."

Bailey looked over at Penelope. They'd been partners last week and rocked it. Penelope pointed to herself, then to Bailey, and smiled. But before Bailey could even stand up, Hannah had dragged her desk over next to Bailey's.

"What do you think we're going to have to do? Are we going to have to do something in front of everyone? That makes me kind of nervous. Even introducing myself I got all embarrassed," Hannah said. "Thanks for helping me out."

"Sure," Bailey answered. Hannah didn't like the idea of doing something in front of other people? Why did Hannah's mom have to sign her up for drama?

Bailey remembered the answer a second later. Hannah's mom had signed her up for drama because she knew that was one of the electives Bailey was in. Bailey had assumed Hannah was at least sort of interested in it herself, though. But now it seemed like she was terrified of the idea of performing.

Bailey leaned close to Hannah. "Don't be nervous. We'll be doing everything together."

"First we're going to do the mirroring warm-up.

Bailey, you can explain it to Hannah," Ms. Healy said. "Go until I say switch."

"Just do everything I do," Bailey said. She stood up. So did Hannah. She raised her arm. So did Hannah. She clapped her hands. So did Hannah. She kicked out her leg. So did Hannah. She opened her mouth as wide as it would go. So did Hannah. She pressed her hands against the sides of her head and pretended to howl in pain. So did Hannah. Hannah was really good at the mirroring game!

"Okay, switch," Ms. Healy called.

Bailey looked at Hannah, waiting for her to move, but she just stood there with her arms at her sides, both feet planted on the floor. "Do anything. Doesn't matter what," Bailey finally whispered.

"I can't think of anything," Hannah whispered back.

Bailey made her mouth move along with Hannah's. Hannah raised her hand. Bailey was relieved. She raised her hand. Hannah clapped her hands. Bailey clapped along with her. Hannah kicked out her leg.

As Bailey imitated the motion, she realized that Hannah was doing everything Bailey had done when Bailey was the leader. *Wow*. She was even more nervous than Bailey had realized. She couldn't even think of new actions to try.

Hannah stretched her mouth open as wide as it would go, continuing to do exactly what Bailey had done. "All right, now we're going to do a little improv scene," Ms. Healy announced. "Stay in your teams."

Bailey glanced over at Penelope. It would be so much more fun to be her partner. But it was good she was paired up with Hannah, since it was probably making her less anxious.

"I'm going to give each team a scene to improvise," Ms. Healy explained. "There's a twist, though. In the scene, you'll both be aliens and you'll speak an alien language. Geep! Gloop adoop ab stog. Like that."

Everybody laughed, except Hannah, who looked like she was getting seasick or something.

"When you do your scene, the rest of us will try to guess what you're doing. You can use gestures, and of course facial expressions and different tones of voice." Ms. Healy began passing around folded slips of colored paper.

Bailey peered over Hannah's shoulder when she opened theirs. It said: *One of you is lost. The other is giving directions.*

"Cool. Which one do you want to be?" Bailey asked.

"Doesn't matter," Hannah said. Bailey wasn't sure,

but she thought Hannah's voice had trembled a little. "You pick."

"You be lost," Bailey said. She thought the lost character might have to talk a little less. Plus it wouldn't matter if Hannah looked sort of scared. It made sense for someone who was really lost to look scared, especially if it was late at night or something.

"I don't know how to make up a language," Hannah confessed.

"Just make sounds, like Ms. Healy did," Bailey said. "It doesn't matter what they sound like. All you have to do is make your voice go up at the end when you're asking a question. And if you're getting upset, you could talk louder and faster. Try it. Try telling me you're lost and you need directions home."

"Beep, beep, beep beep, beep, beep," Hannah said. Each word came out the same. And not just because each word was "beep" either. None of them was louder or softer, and Hannah's face stayed expressionless the whole time.

"Good," Bailey said. "I liked the beeps." She wanted to encourage Hannah. She didn't think Hannah should have signed up for the class just so she'd know somebody in it. But Hannah was here now, and she looked like she had a massive case of stage fright. Bailey wanted to help her out. "Remember how Ms. Healy said we could use gestures and facial expressions? How about if you try it again and do that? And try to make your voice go up at the end of the question when you're asking how to get home. Oh, and maybe try a few words that aren't 'beep.'"

Hannah nodded, then swallowed hard and began. "Eeep beep." She twisted her lips into something that looked like a frown. "Feep fap bleep wap?" She raised her eyebrows.

"Great. You got in some fun alien words. Your voice went up this time." It had gone up a little, although Bailey wasn't sure anyone who didn't know it was supposed to go up would have noticed. "Now—"

Ms. Healy clapped. "Okay, time's up. Which team wants to go first?"

Penelope and her partner, Allison, who had gone to Bailey's elementary school, both raised their hands. Ms. Healy smiled at them. "Come on up to the front. When you think you know what they're talking about, call it out," she told the rest of the class.

Penelope and Allison moved all the way to one side of the room. Then they began to tiptoe across, raising their knees high and pointing their toes. It was like goofy cartoon characters trying to be super sneaky.

Bailey giggled. So did a bunch of other kids.

They stopped, then looked to the left and then to the right. Penelope whispered something to Allison in alien gleeps and gloops. Penelope pretended to open a bag and take something out. She made a twisting motion. Then pulled her arm back. Bailey thought she'd just opened a door.

Penelope crept forward, pretended to reach for something, and put it in a bag. Allison tripped. Penelope gave a "kwerp!" of alarm, then a string of words that sounded like angry scolding.

Allison pressed her hands over her mouth, mumbling what sounded like an apology. Then she pretended to reach for something.

"Burglars!" someone cried out.

"You got it!" Allison answered. She and Penelope gave a bow.

"Great!" Ms. Hardy told them. "I liked how you gave your words emotion. Nice job. Who's next?"

Bailey raised her hand. Hannah tried to pull it back down. "It'll be better to get it over with," Bailey whispered, and Hannah let go.

"Okay, let's get the cousins up here," Ms. Healy said.

The cousins. Bailey liked that. Her grandmother always told stories about all the things she and her cousins did together, but Bailey had never had a relative her age living nearby. Still, she wished Hannah had skipped signing up for drama, since she clearly hated it.

Bailey and Hannah walked to the front of the room. Bailey turned to Hannah and waited for her to begin. She didn't say anything. Bailey waited a beat. Hannah still didn't say anything.

"Ilp tor oop ab yanyan?" Bailey put her hand on Hannah's arm and tried to look concerned. She could feel Hannah's arm trembling.

Hannah gulped but managed to make a few beeps. Bailey launched into what she hoped would look like intricate directions, pointing here, pointing there, squeaking and hooting and honking out words.

Her cousin blinked at her. Bailey tried to make the same gestures and say the same words again, like she was repeating the directions.

Hannah made a few more soft beeps, her face blank, her hands twisted together in front of her. Bailey decided she had to end the scene before Hannah had a full-on panic attack. She tugged Hannah forward, explaining to her in alien speak that she was going to take her home.

"Who wants to take a guess about what was

happening between our two aliens?" Ms. Healy asked.

There was a long, long silence.

"It's a challenging exercise," Ms. Healy said. "Why don't you tell us?" She looked over at Bailey and Hannah.

"She was lost, and I was telling her how to get home," Bailey explained.

"I can see that," Penelope said. "That's why you were doing all the pointing, and why she looked so upset."

"Right," Bailey answered.

"Good effort. Who's next?" Ms. Healy asked.

"Thanks, Bailey," Hannah whispered. "You saved me up there!"

Bailey smiled. "What are cousins for?" she answered.

CHAPTER 5

How to Have an Awesome Party

• • •

1. Choose a theme.
2. Make a guest list.
3. Send invitations.
4. Plan food that matches theme.
5. Plan a few activities, but leave time in between.
6. Buy supplies a few days in advance (including cleaning supplies).
7. Clean.
8. Ask parents for permission (should probably be #1).
9. Decorate the day before.
10. Choose music.
11. Ask for help if you need it.
12. Make sure no one ends up standing alone by themselves (especially Hannah).
13. Make sure to say good-bye to people when they leave.

"How'd Hannah do in school today?" Bailey's mom asked when the family sat down for dinner that night.

Before Bailey could answer, the kitchen door opened and Gus came barging in. "We're having fish. And they still have their eyeballs in their heads. I need to eat here. It's that or starve." He flopped down in the empty chair at the table.

Bailey and Gus had worked out the perfect way of getting out of eating dinners they didn't like, by going to each other's houses anytime fish (Gus) or eggplant (Bailey) was being served.

"Well, we don't want to be arrested for aiding in child famishment," Bailey's father answered. He stood up and got an extra plate and silverware. As soon as he set them down, Gus served himself a pile of spaghetti and two pieces of garlic bread. Bailey's mom added some salad to his plate.

"So, Mom, Dad, I think I need to have a party," Bailey announced.

"Need?" Her father raised an eyebrow, but he was smiling.

"Yes, need," Bailey answered. "Mom, you were asking how Hannah did at school today." She looked over at Gus. "Hannah, in case you forgot to listen when

I talk, like you do half the time, is my cousin who just moved to town."

"Hannah, yeah." Gus used his fingers to pop a meatball into his mouth, then closed his eyes and gave a dreamy smile. He loved meatballs.

"Hannah honestly didn't do that great today," Bailey continued. "She practically had a panic attack in drama. She only took it because she wanted to be in the same class with me. I asked Tess, and Vivi, and Olivia how she was in the classes she was in with them, and they all said she seemed kind of nervous. She needs to get to know more people, so she'll feel more at home. So . . . party!"

Her parents looked at each other. They could have whole conversations without even opening their mouths. "I think that's a great idea," her mom said. Her dad nodded. "When?"

"As soon as possible," Bailey answered. "I'm thinking this Saturday. It doesn't give people a lot of notice, but I can call everybody tonight, then start working on a theme."

"While doing your homework," her father said.

"Of course!" Bailey promised. "Gus, you have to come," she ordered. "And you have to bring a couple boys from your school."

"Boys?" her mom asked. "Since when do you have boys at your party?"

"I'm not in elementary school anymore," Bailey answered. "Gus, you've got your assignment, right?"

"Drag boys to your party," he answered.

"Invite," Bailey corrected. "Invite boys to my incredible party for Hannah."

"Thanks for all your help, Dad. It looks awesome, don't you think?" Bailey asked on Saturday evening. The basement glowed with neon colors under the two black lights her father had put up. Bailey had used glow chalk and a stencil to draw designs on the cement floor, and she'd hung neon posters on the walls.

"Totally awesome, dudette," her father answered in a voice he thought sounded like an LA surfer dude.

Bailey had thought about going with a simple "Welcome Hannah" theme for her party, but had decided on a glow party instead. It just sounded more fun, and it was easier to plan food and games around "glow" than "welcome."

The doorbell rang. "Somebody's here!"

"I hope so," she heard her father say as she raced up the basement stairs. She was almost to the top when she remembered she'd forgotten to turn on the music.

She spun around and almost slammed into her dad.

"See, I remembered I was banned from the basement as soon as anyone gets here—unless I hear things getting out of control," he said.

"Good. Thanks. Will you go turn my iPod on? It's already connected to the minispeaker. Please!" Bailey turned around again and hurried up the stairs. "Then come back up again," she called over her shoulder.

She flung open the front door, expecting to see Olivia. She'd promised to come over a little early, so nobody would feel weird about being first. Instead, it was Hannah on the porch. "You're here! Great!" Bailey exclaimed. The whole point of the party was Hannah!

Bailey had begged until her parents agreed to let her invite twenty people. Even though they hadn't had much notice, almost everyone she'd invited had said yes. She'd phoned, texted, and made a personal visit to Gus to remind him to bring himself and other boys. Tonight was going to be so fun.

"I thought I'd get here a little early in case you needed help," Hannah said.

"Thanks. That's great. I like to be extraprepared, and you can assist." Bailey told her. "I think I have everything pretty much ready to go. In—" She checked her watch. "In ten minutes, it will be time to start bringing food down. You could help with that."

"Sure," Hannah answered. "Oh, look. I got new sneaks. Do you like them?"

"Absolutely," Bailey answered, smiling when she saw they were the same as the sneakers she had on, but in a different color. Her cousin continued to be her style twin. Except Hannah always added a personal touch. Like with the sneakers, she'd added a curlicue of rhinestones on both toes. She was really creative.

"You might want to take them off before you go downstairs, if you want to keep them paint-free," Bailey said. She'd told everyone to wear only clothes they didn't mind getting paint on.

"Right." Hannah slipped them off.

The doorbell rang. This time it was Olivia. "Oh, hi . . . both of you." She was clearly surprised to see Hannah there early. "I thought my assignment was to be here before anyone else." Her eyes flicked to Hannah, then back to Bailey.

"I wanted to be here if Bailey needed help," Hannah answered. "You've got to be extraprepared for a party."

"Exactly!" Bailey exclaimed. "See, Hannah knows." Olivia had said she thought every second of the party didn't need to be planned in advance, but Bailey liked planning, and clearly Hannah did too.

"She sounds exactly like you," Olivia observed.

"I know!" Bailey wrapped an arm around Hannah, then checked her watch again. "It's getting close to go time," she announced. "Oh, you go down to the basement, okay? Get people started on their T-shirts when they come down." Bailey had gotten big white T-shirts that everyone could paint in neon colors. It would look so cool under the black lights. And it was a great icebreaker activity.

"Got it. Do you want to come, Hannah?" Olivia asked.

"I'll stay and help Bailey," Hannah answered.

Olivia raised her eyebrows, and Bailey thought she gave Hannah a weird look.

"Okay, I'll be getting the party started downstairs," Olivia said with a grin, and Bailey decided she was wrong about the weirdness.

A second later, the doorbell rang again. "I'll start bringing down the food," Hannah said. She started to scurry towards the kitchen, but Bailey caught her by the arm.

"Stay with me. I want you to meet everyone," Bailey said. She opened the door. *Yes!* It was Gus, and he had two friends with him. Boy-type friends. "Hannah, this is my next-door neighbor Gus." She stared at Gus until he remembered he should introduce her and Hannah to his friends.

"This is Bryce." He jerked his thumb towards a tall, dark-haired boy. "That's Steven." He jerked his thumb towards a freckled blond boy.

"I'm glad you could come," Bailey told them. "Gus will take you downstairs. That's where we're having the party. My friend Olivia is already down there." She got an idea just as they headed off.

"Wait, Gus." He came back. "Will you bring food down? Hannah said she'd help." She turned to Hannah. "Gus is more like an honorary brother than a neighbor, so I get to put him to work."

Hannah gave him a shy smile. "I guess if you're Bailey's kind-of-brother, that means you're my cousin too."

"I guess so," he told her. He smiled back. He was a good guy.

Bailey squinted at the clock. It was hard to see the numbers with the black light. Almost six. She opened her bag of supplies and pulled out the glow necklaces she'd strung together. She was going to stretch the illuminated rope across the room so they could play volleyball with glow-in-the-dark balloons.

She looked around for Olivia and grinned. Oh and a bunch of other girls were doing model struts up and down the basement, showing off the T-shirts they'd designed with the neon paint. They were all trying to outdo one another with snappy turns, extreme poses, and exaggerated pouts or haughty stares. A couple of the guys had even joined in, and everybody else was yelling encouragement to their favorites.

But where was Hannah? She wasn't doing the model thing, and she wasn't part of the group cheering them on. She wasn't over by the snack table or the drinks. Bailey hoped she hadn't slipped upstairs. Her cousin wasn't very comfortable in crowds.

She should probably go check. Bailey took a few steps towards the stairs, then saw Hannah and Gus sitting on the bottom step, heads close together. Excellent. She'd hoped having them bring down the food together would help them get to know each other a little, and it had worked! Gus could be a pain, but he could also be a good friend. He always showed up when Bailey needed him. Like tonight. It would be great for Hannah to have him for a friend too. She turned around. "Hey, Olivia!" Bailey called. "Come help me hang this up."

Olivia didn't answer. She kept on working the catwalk. It was probably too noisy for her to hear Bailey.

"I got it!" Hannah rushed over.

"Thanks," Bailey said.

"I want to use this to make a volleyball net." She held up the linked necklaces. "I put hooks up yesterday. Can you do this side while I go attach the other one?"

"On it."

As soon as they got the net in place, Bailey got a couple glow-in-the-dark balloons out of the laundry bag where she'd stashed them, then crossed over to the minispeaker and turned down the music a little. "Time for volleyball." She batted one of the balloons into the air. "We're playing hands-free. You can use your hands when you serve, but otherwise it's just feet and head."

"Who wants to be on Team Epic with me and Hannah?" Gus called as he headed over.

Bailey smiled at him. He was really coming through. She'd have to use her mom's recipe to make him as many meatballs as he could eat. Although that could take days.

Olivia stepped next to Bailey. "Do you feel like you're playing Simon Says? I mean Bailey Says?" Olivia said into Bailey's ear.

"What do you mean?" Bailey asked, half her attention on the volleyball game.

"It feels like Hannah's imitating you sometimes, what you wear, what you think is funny," Olivia explained. "Who you're friends with. Like tonight, she's been hanging with Gus almost the whole time. Doesn't it kind of bother you?"

"We just have the same kind of style," Bailey protested. "And I wanted Gus to—" Out of the corner of her eye, Bailey saw a glowing orange balloon coming towards her. She automatically bounced it off her knee, joining in the game.

When they'd played three times, people started heading to the drink table. Bailey headed over too.

"Why'd Olivia have to leave early?" Vivi asked as Bailey did a check on how much ice was left.

"She didn't. She's around somewhere," Bailey answered. Olivia had promised to get to the party early and stay until the very end.

"She left right when we were starting the volleyball game," Vivi answered.

Bailey looked around, then scanned the room more carefully. Vivi was right. Olivia was gone.

CHAPTER 6

How to Have a Great Friendship

· · · ·

1. Do fun things together.
2. Pay attention to what's going on in your friend's life.
3. Stay in touch—even when you get busy.
4. If you're upset with your friend, talk about it. (Talk, not yell!)
5. Be supportive when your friend is going through something hard.
6. Don't keep secrets from your friend.
7. Let your friend know you appreciate them.

Wr o wr is Oh?

Bailey hit send. It was the fourth text she'd sent Olivia since the party ended last night. So far, Olivia hadn't answered any of them. What was going on with her?

"What color should the dragonfly be?" her grandfather asked her and Hannah. He was painting a mural on the wall of Hannah's bedroom, with Hannah and Bailey's help. Bailey had told him once that she'd love a mural of a meadow, and he'd promised he would paint one on all four walls, so she'd be surrounded by flowers every time she slept over, but he hadn't gotten to it. Until now.

He'd offered to paint anything Hannah wanted, but when Hannah had heard Bailey had wanted a meadow, she said she couldn't think of anything better than that.

"What color do you think, Bailey?" Hannah asked.

"Turquoise," she answered. She hadn't needed to think about it at all. She'd pictured the meadow a million times. "But you should have what you want, Hannah," she added quickly, reminding herself that this wasn't her room anymore.

"Perfect!" Hannah exclaimed. "Do you have any silver, Granddad?"

"Silver?" Bailey asked. She hadn't imagined any silver in the mural.

"I, um, thought the veins of the dragonfly's wings might look cool in silver, just thin lines," Hannah explained.

"That would be beautiful," Bailey answered truthfully.

"You have the eye of an artist," Bailey's grandfather—make that Bailey *and* Hannah's grandfather—told Hannah. "Turquoise and silver it is," he said. He opened a small can of turquoise paint.

Bailey felt a little pang when he began filling in the dragonfly he'd sketched on the wall. She carefully closed the can of fuchsia she'd been using to fill in a giant tulip. "I'm thirsty. I'm going to go get something to drink."

"I'll come too," Hannah volunteered.

"That's okay. I'll bring something up for all of us," Bailey answered.

She wanted a few minutes by herself. She was being silly about the mural. It was great that her grandfather was doing it for Hannah. Hannah needed something special. Yeah, Bailey had just thrown a party for her, but it was great her granddad was doing something to make her feel at home here too. Just the way her grandmother had. She'd taken Hannah out shopping for a new comforter and matching curtains.

Bailey went to the kitchen and took three sodas out of the fridge. She didn't feel like going back to her—Hannah's—room yet.

She checked her phone, just to make sure she hadn't noticed Olivia texting her back. But there was no message.

Finally! Baily thought the next morning when she checked her phone and saw there was a text from Olivia. She eagerly opened it.

cnt walk 2 skool 2day. c u there.

Bailey sighed. It felt like it had been forever. They'd hardly hung out at the party. Bailey had been too busy keeping up with the food and organizing the games, and then Olivia had taken off early. Bailey still didn't know why. Well, they'd be able to talk before English.

But Olivia didn't get to class until about thirty seconds before the bell rang. They didn't have time to do more than exchange hi's. Bailey thought about passing her a note, but Mrs. Hahn, their teacher, was kind of strict. If she got caught, she'd be in trouble. She'd have to wait until after class.

"Where were you yesterday?" Bailey burst out as soon as they stepped out into the hall after English ended. "And why'd you leave my party early?"

"I had to run some errands with my mom after church," Olivia answered. She ignored the question about the party.

"You missed helping my granddad work on a meadow mural in Hannah's room," Bailey told her. They both liked helping Bailey's grandfather paint. One year they'd painted a bunch of birdhouses with him, which had gotten put up all over Frank Liske Park.

"He did a meadow mural for Hannah?" Olivia asked.

"She thought it sounded cool," Bailey answered.

"Of course she did." Olivia's eyes narrowed. "She knew it was your idea, right?"

"Yeah, and she thought it would be perfect for the room," Bailey said.

"But *you* loved the meadow idea," Olivia said. "Couldn't your grandfather have done it in your room and done something different in Hannah's?"

"None of us thought of it," Bailey said. She wished she had, but it was too late. It didn't matter. She could come up with another idea—although she'd made a list of fifty-two possibilities before she'd decided a meadow would make the very best mural. She felt a little pang again, like the one she'd had when she saw her grandfather working on the dragonfly. She pushed the feeling away.

"You should have seen how happy Hannah was. She—"

Olivia didn't let her finish. "I have to go. I have gym.

See you!" She strode off before Bailey could even say bye.

Okay, today Olivia and I will finally get to hang out, Bailey thought a week later. She and Oh had joined the Spanish club, and they were going to the first meeting that day at lunch.

It seemed like it had been a billion years since Bailey had gotten a chance to really talk to Olivia. Since she'd gotten to town, Hannah had been with them practically every second they were together. It wasn't that Hannah wasn't nice. But Bailey missed having some best-friend time without her cousin around. She and Olivia didn't have the same kind of convos when Hannah was with them.

They'd texted some, but that wasn't the same. And it seemed like Olivia was always saying she had to study or help take care of her little sister. Bailey knew something was bugging Olivia, and now she'd finally have the chance to find out what.

"¡Hola, chiquita!" Bailey called when she reached Olivia's locker, where they'd agreed to meet up so they could go to the meeting together.

"I was afraid you were going to say a certain peelable

fruit after chiquita," Olivia said, sounding more like the regular Olivia than she had in a while.

"I wouldn't do that to you. I know how you feel about the yellow fruit that shall remain unnamed," Bailey answered.

"Wow, it feels like a billion years since I've talked to you," Olivia commented as they started down the hall. "I know we've talked, but it's just, I don't know, different with Hannah."

"Exactly." It was so great to have a friend who practically shared a brain with you. Someone who knew everything there was to know about what you liked and hated and dreamed about. "So what's up with you? Because I know there's something."

Olivia looked surprised. "You could tell?"

"Of course I could tell," Bailey answered. "I'm your best friend."

"I hope Hannah couldn't," Olivia said.

"Hannah? What's Hannah got to do with anything?" Bailey asked.

"I thought you could tell!" Olivia exclaimed.

"I could tell something was wrong, but I didn't know what. So tell me," Bailey urged.

"It's just . . . I know at the party you said you didn't

think it was weird that Hannah imitates you," Olivia began.

"Because I don't think she is," Bailey said.

"Yeah, she is, and it's weird, Bails," Olivia told her.

"We just ended up liking a lot of the same things," Bailey protested.

"It's more than that. Do you want a Bailey-style list that proves it?" Olivia asked, and Bailey nodded. Olivia held up a finger. "One. She got herself put in almost all your classes."

"But—"

Olivia kept going. She held up a second finger. "Two. She copied your signature style. She wears polka dots every day! And she got the same identical sneakers."

"They were a different color, and—" Bailey started to explain.

Olivia kept right on going, putting up a third finger. "Three. The only friends she has are your friends. Me, Tess, Vivi, and since the party, Gus. Has she ever even talked to anyone you don't know?"

"She must have—"

Olivia charged on, holding up another finger. "Four. She repeats things you say all the time. And whatever you say you like, she says she likes."

"You make it sound so serious," Bailey said.

Olivia pulled in a deep breath, then answered. "I think it might be serious. Maybe she does it because she's so upset about her parents' divorce or because she isn't feeling settled here yet. Maybe it feels, I don't know, safer or easier just to do what you do and hang out with just the people who are already your friends. But whatever reason she's doing it, it's just weird, Bails."

"I think you're making it into more of a big thing than it is," Bailey said. "Like the polka dots. She told us she was into polka dots that day at the mall when she bought the scarf. She liked them before she met me."

"But we don't know that's true," Olivia said slowly. "It's not like you know if she came to town with all those polka-dotted clothes—because she has more than the scarf. She could have gotten them all after she found out you wear polka dots all the time. Was she wearing anything polka-dotted before we went to the mall? Did she have her nails painted with dots, the way she has every day since then? What about the first day she got here?"

Bailey tried to think. She pictured the kitten at Kitty City kneading Hannah's shirt. Bailey was pretty sure the shirt was pale green with little flowers. She didn't think anything else Hannah had been wearing that day had dots either. She closed her eyes, trying to remember more. She could almost see Hannah's hands holding the kitten. She thought she remembered light pink nails with shimmery silver tips.

Slowly Bailey opened her eyes. "She wasn't, was she?" Olivia asked, caramel-colored eyes filled with concern.

"I don't think so, but I'm not positive," Bailey admitted. "But even I don't wear polka dots *every* day. Only almost every day. And I think it was her mom who decided Hannah would like to be in classes with me, not Hannah. And anyway, it's not like we like *all* the same things."

"What about the school pizza? After you said you liked it, Hannah was all 'It's better than the pizza at any of my schools.' But she didn't even eat all of the little piece Tess gave her, so clearly she didn't like it." Olivia began speaking faster. "And there's the thing with Mr. Moya's jokes. When she thought you thought they were funny, Hannah did too. Then you said they were corny, and she backed off and said whatever joke you were talking about wasn't that funny. *Then* you said the jokes were funny because they were corny, and she agreed, like she hadn't just said she didn't think they were funny. And she stayed with Gus—your practically brother—almost every second at your party. And, and! She's having your grandfather paint a meadow mural for her, and that's an idea you came up with."

That stung a little. "I sort of wish she wasn't getting that mural," Bailey admitted.

"She might be imitating you because she's feeling insecure or something," Olivia said. "And I get that. She's going through a lot. But if I were you, it would be making me crazy. It makes me a little crazy just watching. It's like she's taking over your life."

Bailey felt her stomach trying to twist itself into a pretzel. Was Olivia right? She shook her head. "She's not taking over anything. It's just that we like a lot of the same things, including people," Bailey mumbled, knowing she was repeating herself but feeling like she had to defend her cousin. Her phone buzzed almost the instant the words were out of her mouth.

where r u? i'm at our table.

"It's from Hannah," Bailey told Olivia.

Olivia opened her mouth to answer, then shut it.

"She wants to know where I am. She says she's already at our table," Bailey said. "I forgot to tell her about the club meeting." She quickly shot a text back.

going 2 spanish club. see u in track.

"Maybe Hannah will find a club of her own to join," Bailey said as they walked down the hall towards the room where Spanish Club was meeting. "Then she could make some new friends."

"That would be great," Olivia said as they stepped inside and found seats. "But I'm not sure she wants new friends. I think she's happy with yours."

"That's kinda harsh," Bailey said.

"Maybe a little," Olivia admitted.

There wasn't more time to talk, because Señora McAllister had stepped up to the front of the room. "Welcome! It's great to see so many of you here. I know we're going to come up with some great events where we can learn more about the cultures of Mexico and Spain and, of course, have fun!"

One of the boys let out a whoop.

"The first thing you need to do is elect your officers," Señora McAllister told them. "I'll take nominations for—"

The door burst open. Bailey felt her eyes widen when Hannah rushed in. "Sorry I'm late," Hannah told the teacher, her face pink with embarrassment.

She headed directly over to Bailey. "Would you mind moving to that desk so I can sit with my cousin?" she asked Olivia in a low voice.

Olivia looked over at Bailey. There were some questions it was almost impossible to say no to without being rude. Bailey gave a helpless little shrug. Olivia stood up without a word, moved to the empty desk, and sat down.

Bailey didn't get why Hannah was even there. She wasn't taking Spanish.

Bailey hesitated for a few seconds, then took a deep breath and raised her hand, just as Señora McAllister started talking about the election of officers. "Yes?" the teacher said.

"Um, is it okay to be in the Spanish club if you're not taking Spanish?" Bailey asked. Hannah really did need some friends of her own. It wasn't that Bailey didn't want to hang around with her. She just didn't want to be with her every second. She and Olivia needed some time by themselves.

"I don't think that's ever come up before," Señora McAllister answered.

"I'm not taking Spanish this semester," Hannah piped up. "I was taking it at my old school, though, and

I'm a little ahead. The principal said I should start in the second semester. So even though I'm not in Spanish now, I will be soon."

Señora McAllister smiled. "That's fine, then. Welcome to our school. And welcome to Spanish Club. Why don't you introduce yourself?"

"I'm her cousin." Hannah pointed at Bailey.

CHAPTER 7

How to Walk More than One Dog at a Time (for Next Time, Even Though There Probably Won't Be a Next Time)

* * *

1. Walk in a no-squirrel zone.
2. If you're right-handed, hold the leash of the dog that pulls the most in your right hand.
3. Have lots of treats for bribes.
4. Use a different-color leash for each dog, so you know right away which leash controls which dog.
5. Keep your elbows bent and your arms close to your sides. If you let your arms get pulled straight, you could get pulled right off your feet. (This should be moved to #1.)
6. Give the sit command if you feel like you're losing control.
7. Make a list of how to get a dog to obey the sit command.

Bailey was a little relieved when she and Hannah reached the corner where Hannah turned to head to their grandparents' house and Bailey continued straight to get to her house.

Just as she started up her walkway, she heard dogs. A lot of dogs. Some with high yips, some with low woofs, some with hound-dog howls, some with excited whines. She grinned. It was Gus out doing his dog walking.

Maybe she could talk to Gus about the Hannah situation! Suddenly it had become a situation. Bailey already knew what Olivia thought. She needed another opinion. Gus could be surprisingly good at helping with problems.

She broke into a trot, and the dogs got louder when they spotted her coming towards them. "Hi, hi. Hi, hi, hi!" Bailey exclaimed, waving to them. "Hey," she said to Gus. "Want me to take some?" She usually didn't offer. The dogs were sort of hard to control. But since she was here to get his help, she figured she should give him some help too.

He handed her two leashes, one attached to Bruce, a big, slobbery, slow Saint Bernard, and one attached to Franz, a hyper wiener dog. Gus still held the leash for Hans, Franz's brother. It was best to keep them separated if you could. They got very competitive about being the last one to pee on the bushes and trees in the neighborhood.

"I'm not splitting my money with you," Gus warned.

"I know, I know. I didn't think you'd recently had a personality transplant," Bailey joked. Gus always had something he was saving his cash for—some first-edition comic, or a new piece of electronics equipment, or new special-effects makeup for the monster movies he was always making.

"So what do you want then? Because I know you're not a dog person," Gus said. It was true. She was more of a cat girl. He volunteered at the Moss Street shelter and had convinced her to go with him once. She hadn't even lasted an hour. Too much noise. And drool.

"And you're not much of a people person," she shot back. He was clearly in annoying almost-brother mode today, instead of fun almost-brother. Still, he was the only almost-brother she had. "Actually, I wanted to ask you something."

"Yeah?"

"Okay, so, Olivia thinks my cousin Hannah is copying me," Bailey told him. "Here's the deal. She *is* in four of my classes, but that's because her mom asked the school to put her in them. Also, she just joined the Spanish club, like me."

"So?"

"There are other things too, like she always wears polka dots like me, and she thinks the same things are funny that I do, and sometimes she repeats things I say. And she's having my grandfather paint her room the way I wanted it when it was my room, you know, when it was the room I always had when I slept over. Do you think it's weird?"

Gus opened his mouth to answer, but before she could, Monsieur, the poodle he was walking, saw a squirrel and lunged for it, cutting in front of Bruce. Bailey had to duck under Monsieur's leash to avoid being decapitated. Then she had to unwind Franz's leash. Somehow it had gotten wrapped three times around one of his back legs.

"Somebody should make a device that makes squirrels invisible to dogs," Gus muttered.

"Maybe that should be your next project." Gus was always fooling around with inventions.

Gus snorted. "You actually think that's possible?" He shook his head.

"So getting back to my problem, do you think it's weird? Or normal?" Bailey asked.

"Hannah seemed cool at the party. I don't get why it's bugging you," Gus told her.

"Here's the real question. I think I want to have some time with Olivia and my other friends without Hannah. Especially because she's sort of started to make Olivia a little crazy. But I don't want to hurt Hannah's feelings. Because, really, nothing she's doing is bad. Like you said, she's cool. So is it okay for me to do things without her sometimes? Yes or no?"

"Although maybe some kind of spray that blocks the scent . . . ," Gus mumbled. He got what Bailey thought of as his mad-scientist expression. "Scent is more important to dogs than sight."

"Focus," Bailey snapped at him. "Me not wanting to hurt Hannah's feelings. Like on Olivia's birthday!" She couldn't believe she'd forgotten even for a few minutes that Olivia's birthday was that weekend. She and Oh always spent their birthdays together, and there was no way Hannah could come. Not now that Bailey knew how much Hannah annoyed Olivia. "It would ruin the whole day if Hannah came with us. But how am I supposed to tell her that?"

"Don't," Gus said. "It's not actually necessary to tell everyone everything. For example, I really didn't need to hear any of this." He shot her a teasing grin and she gave him a somewhat light punch on the arm.

"It's not that easy. Hannah always texts me, asking where I am. She wants to sit next to me every day at lunch. And she and her mom come over to my house a lot," Bailey told him.

"So it shouldn't be a big deal that you do something without her. It's not like you ignore her or anything. You gave her that party," Gus said. "Can't you just explain that you and Olivia always do your birthdays by yourselves? Your other friends don't care."

"Maybe. Yeah, I think this might be one of the rare times you're right," she joked. She felt Franz's leash go taut and realized he'd stopped to pee on the Bakers' garbage can.

"You're not supposed to let them pee on people's stuff," Gus told her.

"He didn't ask my permission," Bailey shot back. She gave a tug on Franz's leash. He took a couple of steps but didn't stop peeing. Suddenly Hans realized what was going on. He scrambled right over Monsieur's back and started peeing over the spots Franz had already marked.

"Come on, guys. Come," Bailey called, walking forwards and hoping Franz would follow. Bruce was already happily plodding forwards. But Franz, who probably weighed only about twenty pounds, seemed to have glued himself to the sidewalk. Bailey pulled on the leash, and Franz skittered forwards, his nails fighting to cling to the cement.

"Don't drag him like that," Gus yelled.

"Well, he won't walk," Bailey answered.

Gus slapped his thigh. "Franz, giddyap," he cried. And Franz giddyapped. But first he went through Bailey's legs and around one ankle. She stumbled and landed hard on one knee. She was going to get a bruise as big as the ones Tess always had from falling off her board when she was practicing a new trick. Cats never knocked you to the ground!

"Give them back." Gus sounded exasperated. With her. Not with the insane wiener dog.

Bailey handed back the leashes. They were in front of her house. "See you," she said. "And thanks."

Gus grunted in response, then said, "Have fun with Olivia. I'll just be home crying into my pillow because you didn't ask me to come."

Bailey was still laughing when she walked into the house. "Mom!" she called. Her mother would be able to help her figure out exactly how to explain why

Bailey and Olivia wanted to celebrate Olivia's birthday without Hannah—without hurting Hannah's feelings! She'd understand why Olivia's birthday absolutely had to be a Hannah-free zone.

"In the kitchen," her mom called back.

"I need to ask you a—" she began as soon as she entered the kitchen. She cut herself off when she saw that her aunt Caitlin was sitting at the table with her mom. Obviously she wasn't going to be able to bring up her Hannah problem now. "It's a homework thing. We can talk about it later. Hi, Aunt Caitlin."

"Sit down with us for a minute," her aunt said. "I wanted to thank you for being so great to Hannah. She really appreciates the way you introduced her to all your friends. She said all of them have been so friendly. I appreciate it too."

Bailey nodded. "It must be hard starting at a new school."

"It is. Especially because Hannah really didn't want to move. She's had so many upsets lately. On top of . . . of the divorce, moving was almost too much. She'd barely started at the last school." Aunt Caitlin's brow furrowed with worry. "Every time her dad talks to her on the phone, she gets so sad. I try to talk to her about it, but she shuts me down. The only time she seems really happy is when she tells me about things she's doing with you."

"I'm glad she's living here," Bailey said truthfully, her mind whirling. She needed to figure out how to get in some best-friend time with Olivia, especially on her birthday. That was vital.

But Hannah was her cousin. She needed Bailey. And there was no way Bailey was deserting her.

CHAPTER 8

How to Help Hannah
Deal with Her Parents' Divorce

● ● ●

1. If she wants to talk, let her. Don't push her to talk.
2. Be a good listener.
3. Watch a funny movie together.
4. Be positive.
5. Ask if she needs help with homework/do homework together.
6. Give her a compliment.
7. Make her a snack in case she's too upset to eat.

"Hi! I brought you a bagel with peanut butter." Bailey thrust the foil-wrapped snack into her cousin's hand as soon as Hannah answered the door the next morning. A blog she'd read said when people are upset they sometimes forget to eat and that makes them feel worse.

The bagel was part of Bailey's plan to give Hannah some extra attention. She figured if she did, then Hannah would know Bailey cared about her and was her friend, not just her cousin, even if Bailey didn't invite her to Olivia's All-Day Birthday Adventure, as she and Olivia had been calling it since they were kids. Maybe they'd even be able to do some other stuff without Hannah once in a while. All she had to do was make sure Hannah knew Bailey was always going to be around if Hannah needed her.

She'd decided not to tell Hannah in advance that she'd be out with Olivia on Saturday. If it came up—like if Hannah asked if she and Bailey could do something that day—Bailey would just explain about the birthday tradition. Hannah would understand. Like Gus said, Bailey and Olivia's other friends didn't get offended when she and Oh did things by themselves.

"Thanks." Hannah slid the bagel into her backpack. "I'll have it later. I just finished breakfast. Grandma made her granola."

"With dried mango pieces?" Bailey asked. Her grandmother loved to experiment with different kinds of granola. She and Bailey made it together on mornings when Bailey had spent the night.

"It was yogurt-coated cashews today," Hannah

answered. Bailey had never had that one before. She felt a tiny zing of jealousy, then reminded herself that she'd had tons of time with her grandparents and Hannah had hardly had any.

They started down the sidewalk towards Olivia's. Her house was a little out of the way, but she and Bailey always walked to school together. "Your hair looks great today, Hannah," Bailey said.

Hannah smiled. "Really?" She threaded her fingers through her long blond hair, and Bailey had to glance away so she didn't have to look at the white polka dots painted on Hannah's nails, the main coat of each nail a different color.

Now that Olivia had made her remember Hannah wasn't wearing polka dots on her nails the day she got to town, Bailey couldn't stop wondering if Hannah had been lying about how she was a huge polka dot fan.

Bailey was seriously considering changing her signature look. Except she was afraid Hannah would copy whatever new one she came up with, and that would make Olivia's head go *splat*! It would make Bailey feel weird too.

"Yeah, it's so shiny," Bailey said. "And I love that hair band."

"Thanks," Hannah answered. "I made it by braiding

together strips from an old T-shirt."

"You're a DIY fashionista," Bailey said. "You come up with so much great stuff." She really did.

"I'll make you one if you want," Hannah volunteered. She sounded happy. Good. That was what Bailey wanted.

By the end of the day, she'd gotten through her whole list. Hannah hadn't brought up the divorce, but Bailey had been prepared, ready to be a good listener.

By the time she and Hannah were walking to school together on Friday, Bailey had gotten through most of the list eight more times. The funny movie item wasn't one that she could do every day, so she'd thrown in a couple of extra compliments and found a few jokes online to tell Hannah.

It felt good to be helping her cousin. It wasn't like it was a huge chore. Hannah could be fun. She had great stories about all the places she'd lived—if you coaxed them out of her. And during one of the movies, she'd helped Bailey do a reverse appliqué on one of her T-shirts, cutting out leaves, then sewing a piece of another T-shirt underneath so it showed through. Actually, she'd done the appliqué herself while Bailey watched.

Now that Bailey had given Hannah a lot of extra

attention, she could enjoy spending all day Saturday hanging out with Olivia with a clear conscience. It was Olivia's birthday, and they were going to have some serious fun!

Olivia caught up to Bailey right before she walked into the cafeteria that day at lunch. "I came up with a way to show you that Hannah is copying you on purpose," she announced, her brown eyes gleaming.

"I told you, we just happen to like a lot of the same things," Bailey said. "You and I like a lot of the same things too. That's why we're friends."

"I knew you'd say that. I know you think she just likes the same people you like and the same things you like because you two are soul cousins or whatever," Olivia answered. "But I finally figured out how to show you it's more than that."

"How?"

"You'll see. Come on." Olivia led the way into the cafeteria.

Bailey watched her best friend carefully as they bought food and sat down with Vivi, Tess, and Hannah. What was Olivia planning to do?

Olivia started eating her lunch, chatting about some movie she wanted to see, acting totally normal. Had her plan started? What *was* her plan? Bailey was feeling so jittery that it was hard to sit still.

"I'm going to run to the bathroom." Olivia gave Bailey a look that Bailey knew meant "Come with me."

"I'll come with," Bailey said.

Hannah scrambled to her feet. "I need to go too. I'll go with you."

Olivia raised her eyebrows at Bailey. That couldn't be what Olivia had been talking about, could it? It was totally normal to go to the bathroom with your friends.

After she, Hannah, and Olivia were out of the bathroom stalls and had washed their hands, Olivia pulled her favorite tinted lip balm out of her bag. "I forgot to give this back to you," she said to Bailey. Before Bailey could say the balm wasn't hers, Olivia continued. "Oh, wait. I forgot you gave it to me because you ended up not liking the color. You said you like darker pink. I decided it was a little too pale for me too. Do you want it, Hannah?" She pulled off the top so Hannah could see the shade.

This had to be part of Olivia's plan. First, the lip balm *was* hers, not Bailey's. Second, she *loved* the color. She called it pinktastic.

Hannah shook her head. "It's not really my color either," she said, even though she was wearing a pale pink gloss that was almost exactly the shade of the lip balm Olivia had offered her.

"It isn't?" Olivia asked. "But you wear almost that color all the time. You're wearing it *right now*. That's why I thought you'd want it."

"I, um, bought it by mistake," Hannah said quickly. "It looked darker in the tube. I wanted to throw it away, but my mom won't let me. She . . . she says it's perfectly good and it's wasteful not to use it. That's why I've been wearing it so much. I, uh, I wanted to use it all up as fast as I could so I could buy the color I really like." She nodded four times, then smiled at Olivia. "Thanks for offering it to me, though."

"Sure." Olivia was answering Hannah, but looking at Bailey.

Bailey understood. Olivia had been showing her that Hannah had liked the color until Bailey had said she *didn't* like it. Hannah wasn't a very good actress. It had been so clear she was lying when she told them about buying the wrong color.

Maybe Olivia was right. Maybe Hannah had been copying Bailey from the beginning, starting with buying that polka-dotted scarf. No, even before that. Starting with getting herself in almost every class Bailey was in.

A whooping sound caught Bailey's attention. "Hey,

do you hear that?" Bailey exclaimed. She didn't want to think about Hannah anymore right then. "It sounds like the cheerleaders are doing a pep rally!" She hurried out of the bathroom and back to their table, Hannah right behind her, with Olivia trailing after them.

"Homecoming Day is almost here. And this is reason enough to cheer!" the eighth-grade cheerleaders were chanting. Then they all did kicks or jumps.

"Woo!" Bailey shouted as she applauded.

"Woo!" Hannah cried.

She's like a parrot! Bailey thought, then told herself that half the kids in the caf had yelled "Woo!" at the same time Hannah had.

"Okay, everybody," the head cheerleader called. "We're so excited because you know what happens in two weeks?"

"Homecoming!" the other cheerleaders shouted.

"And right before that?" the head cheerleader cried.

"Spirit Week!" the others yelled in response.

"That's right!" The head cheerleader grinned at the crowd. "For all you sixth graders, East Concord Middle School has the most awesome Spirit Week. There are games during each lunch period and costume competitions, and everybody has fun. This year each grade will pick a Most Valuable Player at the end of the week, and that person will get two free tickets to the Katy Perry concert in Charlotte." She jumped into a split and touched her toes. "The sold-out concert!"

How cool would it be to see Katy Perry live? Bailey's fingers were itching to start a list. With enough planning, she thought she might be able to get chosen as the MVP for the whole sixth grade!

"I love Katy Perry!" Bailey cried.

"Love, love, love her!" Hannah exclaimed.

Is that even true? Bailey wondered, eyeing Hannah. *Or is she saying it only because I said it first?*

Bailey was so glad to get home after school that day. She didn't think she could stand one more second with Hannah. When she'd thought she and Hannah liked a ton of the same things, it had been cool. But now that she knew Hannah was only pretending to like the things Bailey liked, it was weird. Make that annoying. Really annoying.

At least tomorrow would be a completely Hannah-free day. She pulled the Olivia's All-Day Birthday Adventure list out of the front pocket so she could review it. "Mom, you remember we're leaving to pick up Olivia for breakfast at nine, right?" she asked as she headed into the living room.

Her mom put down the book she was reading for her book club. "Of course I remember. You've left me a note by the coffeepot the last two mornings."

Bailey smiled. "You never skip coffee, that's why I put my important messages there."

"I was talking to your aunt Caitlin today, and I told her Hannah was welcome to go with you and Olivia," her mom said. Like it was no big thing.

"Mom, no!" Bailey wailed. "Olivia and I do all our special birthday things. It won't be the same with someone else there."

"I'm sure the three of you will have a great time. Hannah will love everything you have planned," her mother answered.

Or she'll pretend to, Bailey thought. *Since she's trying to turn herself into me—and get my room and my friends and my life, just like Olivia said.*

"You have to tell Aunt Caitlin you were wrong," Bailey told her mother. "It will ruin everything if Hannah comes. And it's not like I've been ignoring her. I've been spending practically every second with her since she moved here. I eat lunch with her every day. She came over to watch a movie this week and last week. She sat with me in Spanish Club. Every time we have to do an acting exercise with a partner, I'm her partner.

We run together every time we have track. I gave her that party! I introduced her to all my friends. I even let her have my idea for the meadow mural, and I really wanted it for myself! I gave her all these compliments and made her a peanut butter bagel."

"I know, honey, but—" her mother began.

"No!" Bailey burst out, interrupting her. "Hannah can come over on Sunday. She can come over every day after school for the rest of my entire life. She can start wearing clothes right out of my closet. She can dye her hair to match mine if she wants to. She can change her name to Bailey. But she can't come with us on Olivia's birthday. She can't! She—"

"Bailey, stop." Now it was her mother who interrupted. "Sit down and listen to me." Her mother looked at Bailey until Bailey gave a reluctant nod and flopped down on the living room sofa.

"It turns out that tomorrow is Hannah's dad's birthday too," Mom said, brushing Bailey's hair away from her face. "Hannah and her mom and dad always did something together on his birthday, just the way you do with Olivia."

"It's not the same," Bailey protested.

"It's very much the same," her mother insisted. "It's

a tradition, just the way you and Olivia celebrating your birthdays together is a tradition. Think how you'd feel celebrating your birthday without Olivia."

"But it's not Hannah's birthday." Bailey wasn't giving in on this one. She wasn't. She'd done everything she could think of to be nice to Hannah, and she'd keep on doing everything. But just not tomorrow.

"Hannah's really missing her dad," Bailey's mother told her. "She's going to be thinking about him so much tomorrow, missing him extrahard. Going out with you and Olivia would help keep her mind off being so far away."

"Why can't she go out with her mom?" Bailey asked. "Why can't they do something together?"

"Aunt Caitlin said she offered to do anything Hannah wanted to, but Hannah said no. Maybe it's because it would make her miss her dad even more if the two of them did something on a day the three of them always spent together. There'd be so many memories, you know?"

Bailey reluctantly nodded.

"Doing something with you and Olivia wouldn't have any old memories connected to it. Hannah could just have fun," her mother went on. "What do you say?"

"I don't really have a choice, do I?" Bailey muttered.

Her mother sighed. "I'm not going to force you," she finally answered. "But I want you to try to put yourself in Hannah's place before you decide."

CHAPTER 9

How Not to Be Annoyed by a Sort-of-Annoying Person

◆ ◆ ◆

1. If it's something small, let it go.
2. Talk to someone about it.
3. Practice saying nice things in the mirror.
4. Smile—faking a smile can actually make you feel happy (according to Dad, at least).
5. Imagine something happy while she's being annoying.
6. Remember that she's not TRYING to be annoying.
7. Relax!!!!!!

"I'm proud of you, Bailey," her mother said after they got in the car the next morning.

"Thanks," Bailey mumbled. She and Olivia had talked last night. Bailey had admitted that Olivia was right about Hannah copying her. She'd also admitted that now that she'd realized Hannah was doing it, it was completely annoying.

But they'd both still decided they had to invite Hannah to spend the day with them. They wouldn't be able to have any fun if they knew Hannah was home by herself, wishing she was with her dad.

Hannah was waiting on the sidewalk when they turned the corner onto her street. "Thanks for inviting me," Hannah said to Bailey when she got in the car.

"Sure." Bailey gave a smile that she hoped didn't look as fake as it felt. She didn't mention Hannah's father. She wasn't sure Hannah would want her to know it was his birthday too. She'd let Hannah bring it up. Or not.

It took only about forty-five seconds to get to Olivia's. Olivia was already waiting out front too. Bailey grinned when she saw her, a real grin. Yeah, Bailey was still a little disappointed that Hannah had to come today, but nothing could make Olivia's birthday less than great.

"First stop, Family Restaurant!" Bailey exclaimed.

"Where they have pancakes as big as your head. Seriously. As. Big. As. Your. Head," Olivia added.

"We always go there on Oh's birthday," Bailey told Hannah.

"It's a day of many traditions. They do all the best things from birthdays past," Bailey's mom said.

"Some of them might seem a little dumb," Olivia admitted. "But we still love them."

"I bet they aren't dumb," Hannah answered.

Bailey and Olivia looked at each other and laughed. "Oh, no. They are," Bailey said. Then she and Olivia laughed some more.

"Don't worry. I'll have them seat me in the back room," Bailey's mom announced as she pulled into the crowded parking lot. "Come get me when you're ready to go."

"Come on!" Bailey cried. She, Olivia, and Hannah rushed into the restaurant. Bailey planted one hand on the hostess stand and with her other hand passed the hostess the note she'd written. "There are three of us."

"Right this way," the hostess said.

"Can we have the booth under the Elvis picture?" Olivia asked. The Family Restaurant was decorated with pictures of old stars, like Elvis and Lucille Ball. They'd sat under Elvis for all of Olivia's birthday celebrations.

"I don't see why not," the hostess answered. She ushered them to the booth.

Bailey fingered the tear in the red vinyl of the seat. It had been there the first time they'd come here for Olivia's birthday breakfast, even though that was years ago. She loved how it was just the same.

After they ordered their drinks, it got really quiet at the table. Olivia and Bailey never had trouble coming up with stuff to talk about. But now Bailey felt really self-conscious sitting there with Hannah. She didn't want to say something and have Hannah go all parrot and repeat it. It would make Olivia crazy. Bailey too.

"Somebody say something!" Olivia finally burst out.

"Um, how's karate going?" Bailey asked.

"Good. I've found a sport where it doesn't matter if you break stuff," Olivia answered. "You're *supposed* to break stuff."

"Awesome!" Bailey said.

"So awesome!" Hannah breathed.

Bailey crumbled her napkin into a tight ball. Why couldn't Hannah at least chose a different word? It's not like there weren't synonyms for "awesome." Her dad, the crossword puzzle fiend, could probably come up with twenty of them off the top of his head.

"Are you into karate?" Olivia asked.

"No," Hannah admitted. "But it sounds awesome."

Bailey noticed Olivia's jaw tighten before she gave Hannah a smile. Hannah was annoying her, but Olivia wasn't going to let it show. Neither was Bailey.

Silence fell again. Bailey's brain went blank. This

felt so weird. Like she and Olivia were in a play and Hannah was the audience. Maybe because Hannah didn't really join in. She just reacted.

"I like that shirt, Hannah," Olivia told her. Last night, Bailey had mentioned that she'd been giving Hannah compliments as part of helping her deal with her parents' divorce. Olivia had clearly decided to join in.

For once, Hannah wasn't wearing something that looked like it was part of Bailey's wardrobe. That was a good sign.

"Thanks," Hannah said. "It's new. My mom took me to the mall." She turned to Bailey. "We got you one too! I forgot to bring it, but I'll give it to you when you drop me off."

Seriously? Seriously! Bailey took a long gulp of orange juice to keep herself from giving a screech of impatience. She couldn't make herself say thank you.

"Did you already do the history homework?" Olivia asked Hannah.

Bailey had also said that she'd been checking in with Hannah about schoolwork. Olivia had decided she would do that too.

"Not yet," Hannah answered.

"Me neither," Olivia said.

And then . . . silence.

"Oh, can you believe Spirit Week is almost here?" Bailey cried. "It's going to be so fun."

"So fun," Hannah agreed. She was repeating Bailey even more than usual. Was it because she was upset, thinking about her dad?

"So fun," Olivia said. A little sarcasm had crept into her voice, but Bailey didn't think Hannah would have noticed.

And then . . . more silence. Way too much silence.

"Remember last year when—" Bailey started, then broke off. It wasn't polite to talk about stuff that had happened when Hannah wasn't around. Before she could think of another topic, the sound of people singing "Happy Birthday" started up.

Bailey grinned as a parade of waiters and waitresses headed towards their booth. Their waitress was in the lead, and she carried a plate of chocolate chip pancakes with eleven candles on them. The hostess had come through!

Bailey and Hannah joined in the singing. When the song wrapped, everyone in the place clapped as Olivia blew out the candles. "Woo!" Bailey cheered.

"Woo!" Hannah echoed.

"They're especially excellent with strawberry syrup,"

Bailey said when they each had a plate of the pancakes in front of them. She poured the syrup over her pancakes and offered the pitcher to Hannah. Hannah poured a few drops on her pancakes, then handed the pitcher to Olivia.

"Don't you like syrup?" Olivia asked Hannah.

"I'm not that much of a strawberry person," she answered. "But it sounded good with chocolate chips, so I decided to try it," she added quickly. She took a bite and nodded enthusiastically. "Good."

"Want some more?" Olivia held out the pitcher.

"No!" Hannah said loudly. She lowered her voice. "I'm good."

"Wait. You had strawberry cookies at my house," Bailey said. She remembered because she'd made the star cookies especially for Hannah and Aunt Caitlin. "You said you loved them."

"I like them sometimes," Hannah answered. "Like those cookies and this syrup."

Bailey looked at the three drops of strawberry syrup on Hannah's pancakes. She was lying. Again.

"You don't have to have it just because we're having it," she burst out. "It's obvious you don't like it. Get maple, get blueberry, get something you actually want to eat."

"I think it will be good with this kind of pancake," Hannah answered, flushing. "These really are as big as your head," she added softly.

"Yeah," Bailey said.

"Yeah," Olivia said.

Then they continued to eat. In silence.

"I know it's for little kids, but we always ride the train on Oh's birthday," Bailey said when her mom pulled into the lot in front of the park.

"Every year we add in something we did the year before," Olivia explained. "The train is what we did the first year we celebrated my birthday together."

"Oh. Cool!" Hannah said.

They bought tickets at the snack shack, then got in line with a bunch of little kids with their parents. Bailey remembered how, the year before, she and Olivia had already been giggling hysterically at this point. But she had that feeling of being watched by an audience again, and it made her feel self-conscious and a little silly.

A cute teenage boy took their tickets. Did he think they were riding the train for serious? Did he think they didn't realize they were too old?

The little seats weren't big enough to hold all three of them. When Bailey slid on, her knees pressing hard against the front of the car, Hannah sat next to her, so Olivia had to sit behind them. Bailey twisted around to smile at her friend. Olivia smiled back, but the smile looked a little fake. Was she feeling weird about being on the train too?

Bailey decided she wasn't going to let Hannah spoil this. When the train started up, Bailey and Olivia waved good-bye to the teenage boy. So did Hannah. Bailey and Olivia waved to every person they saw walking on the path that wound through the park, just the way they did every year. Hannah waved at everyone too.

She looked dorky. Completely dorky. Was that how Bailey and Olivia looked? Bailey's arm suddenly felt heavy. Her hand too. It felt like a strain to wave so hard.

"It's her birthday!" Bailey yelled, pointing back at Olivia. "Say happy birthday to her!"

A little boy and his parents all yelled "Happy birthday," and Bailey felt a little bit of the goofy pleasure that had made her and Olivia laugh all through the ride last year. But only a little bit.

Then Hannah pointed at Olivia and shouted "It's her birthday!" to a couple of teenagers. They stared back blankly, like they were trying to figure out if Hannah was talking to them, and if she was, then why.

Bailey let herself sink down a little in the seat, her

knees coming up almost high enough to hide her face. She was so ready to get off.

"What now?" Hannah asked when the little train pulled into the station.

"We go to a movie at the Gem," Bailey answered as she climbed out of the seat. "We can walk over there. We have some time before it starts. Want to look at the book table?" she asked Olivia.

"Of course," Olivia said. "The library has a table of books for a dime each. Sometimes it has good stuff," she explained to Hannah. They were always having to explain things to Hannah.

"What movie are we seeing?" Hannah asked as they cut through the park.

"We don't know," Bailey admitted. "My dad looked up the times. He told me when the first one started, but that's it."

"We always go to the Gem, so it doesn't matter. Whatever's there, that's what we go to," Olivia explained.

Hannah looked back and forth between Bailey and Olivia, her forehead crinkling. Then she gave a smile that looked like something she'd do in an acting exercise, forced and fake. "Oh. Cool."

"The Gem is always fun," Bailey told her. "It always has these old cartoons, like from the sixties, first."

"And it has these great bird murals up on the front, and a real curtain in front of the screen. It's kind of old-timey," Olivia added.

"Oh. Cool," Hannah said. She kept saying that, but she didn't sound very excited.

Doesn't matter, Bailey told herself. *It's Olivia's birthday. Who cares what Hannah thinks?* Although maybe it was kind of silly to go see a movie when it might turn out to be something really bad that you had no interest in seeing in the first place. For the past two years they'd had good luck, though. They'd added going to a movie on Olivia's ninth birthday.

"Then after that, bowling," Olivia told her. "We even use the bumpers like we did the first time."

We probably look really stupid too, Bailey thought.

"Oh. Cool," Hannah said.

Bailey looked at her watch. She'd never wanted Olivia's birthday to end, but today it had barely started and she was already wishing she could go home.

When she looked up, she caught Olivia checking the time on her cell.

By the time Bailey finally got home, she was exhausted. She went straight to her room and flopped down on the bed, letting her head hang over the edge. She let out a long, long, *long*, loooong sigh.

Having fun on Olivia's birthday had actually felt like work. Bailey had started counting the times Hannah said "Oh. Cool." *Eleven*. It turned out to be eleven. One for every year of Olivia's life.

Olivia's birthday was usually one of Bailey's favorite days of the year. And Hannah had ruined it. She hadn't done it on purpose, but she'd still completely ruined it.

CHAPTER 10

How to Cheer Up After a Hard Day

• • •

1. Take a bubble bath.
2. Listen to music.
3. Watch baby animal videos.
4. Make a list of things you love.
5. Watch a funny movie.
6. Clean out your closet.
7. Read a sad book to make you feel better about your life.
8. Have a Cheerwine.

Bailey needed to talk to Olivia. When a girl's world felt like it had started spinning the wrong way, she needed to talk to her best friend.

But Olivia was gone all day Sunday. She and

her family went to Asheville to visit Olivia's great-grandmother, since she always wanted to give Olivia her birthday present in person.

Olivia was at school on Monday, but so was Hannah. Hannah was the thing Bailey needed to talk to Olivia about! So even though she saw Olivia, it didn't count as actual Olivia time.

And today Olivia had to buy a new gi before karate class, because her little sister, Rose, had colored all over her old one with a felt-tip marker.

So the only thing she could do was pick something from her list of things to do to cheer up after a bad day. She wasn't sure any of them would work after a whole bunch of bad days, though, and that's what Bailey had had. She'd been miserable pretty much since Olivia had given Hannah the lip-gloss test to prove that what Hannah really wanted was Bailey's life.

Bailey decided to go for cleaning her closet first. Having an extremely well-organized closet always made her feel good. As she headed to her room, she tried to decide if she should group her shirts by sleeve length. Right now they were grouped by color, from lightest to darkest. Possibly she could still keep each color together, but within that color, put the shirts with the same sleeve length together, from shortest to longest.

Having a project made her feel a tiny bit better, and she eagerly flung open her closet door, ready to get to work. But what she saw inside made her slam the closet shut again. Polka dots. Her closet was filled with clothes with polka dots—organized by the background color, not the dot color.

She couldn't stand to look at anything dotted right now. Polka dots made her think of Hannah, and thinking of Hannah could not possibly cheer her up.

Okay, it was time for cute animal videos. Bailey hurried over to her desk and powered up her computer and then jumped straight to the Emergency Cuteness YouTube channel she'd made for herself. She clicked on the first one. It showed the fluffiest calico kitten with the biggest eyes curling up next to an extremely shaggy sheepdog for a nap.

So, so cute! Except the kitten made Bailey think of Kitty City, which made her think of Hannah getting all blotchy. She probably didn't even like kittens!

Bailey headed into the kitchen and grabbed a Cheerwine from the fridge, then put it back. Now when she thought of Cheerwine, she thought of the day at the mall when she and Olivia had explained to Hannah what the drink was.

Even when Hannah was blocks away, she was

113

ruining stuff Bailey loved!

Bailey thought about taking a bath. That couldn't possibly make her think of Hannah, but then she caught sight of the kitchen clock and realized it was late enough for Olivia to be done with karate class.

yo, oh. What do you know? Bailey texted.

just out of karate, she texted back.

Boing! The perfect plan appeared in Bailey's head. Olivia's karate dojo was right on Main Street. She'd be walking home. Bailey would surprise her by showing up, and they could walk partway home together. They wouldn't have a lot of time. They'd both have to be home for dinner. But they could have a little time to talk, face-to-face.

don't walk + text, Bailey advised.

Olivia could be a little accident-prone.

k. l8r, Olivia answered.

Bailey spun around and broke into a trot. She reached Main Street just in time to see Olivia coming out of karate in her spotless, for now, white gi. The outfit was so cool-looking it always made Bailey want to take karate. Except she didn't like hitting stuff.

Olivia started down the street away from Bailey— the opposite direction from her house. What was she doing? Maybe she had an errand to do before she went home, Bailey decided. "Oli—"

Bailey only got half the name out before Olivia headed into Gianni's. That was why she had headed the wrong way. She probably wanted something to drink. Bailey would get something too.

What? Bailey skidded to a stop in front of Gianni's big front window. Olivia was sitting at one of the tall tables with Vivi and Tess. They were all laughing.

It felt like her lungs had been ironed flat. Bailey couldn't get any air in. She had to get away from there. She couldn't let them see her. That would be humiliating. If they'd wanted her with them, they would have texted her.

But before she could move away from the window, Vivi spotted her. She leaned over and knocked on the glass. Then they all waved, smiling. "Come in!" Olivia mouthed.

Maybe she was wrong. Maybe they hadn't planned to meet up without her. Maybe Vivi and Tess were already at Gianni's and Olivia came in after karate and saw them. Just the way Bailey was seeing them now.

Yeah, that made sense. Bailey's lungs filled with wonderful air. She waved back to her friends and joined them inside.

"I'm sorry!" Olivia immediately exclaimed.

"Sorry for what?" Bailey asked.

Olivia flushed and didn't answer. "Sorry we didn't invite you," Tess said. She flipped her finger against the wheel of her skateboard and set it spinning. The board was propped up against her stool.

"Me too," Vivi added.

"It's my fault," Olivia admitted. "I asked them to meet me. I had to talk to someone about, you know, how we went out for my birthday and . . ."

She didn't finish, so Bailey finished for her. "And Hannah ruined it."

Olivia nodded.

"Almost all she ever does is agree with something you said, Bails. It's sketchy," Tess said.

"It *is* strange," Vivi agreed. "It's like she's tofu. She doesn't have any flavor of her own. It's almost like she'd just sit there saying nothing and doing nothing if you weren't around for her to copy."

"I would have told you we were meeting up," Olivia said. "But I thought your mom would have made you invite Hannah."

"She might have," Bailey admitted. She was still trying to take in the fact that her friends had left her out.

"Well, you're here now!" Olivia patted the chair next

to her. "Sit down!"

Before Bailey could, her phone rang. She checked the screen. "My mom," she told her friends.

"Where are you?" her mother demanded as soon as Bailey answered. "I just called your grandmother's and you aren't there."

"I'm at Gianni's with Olivia and Tess and Vivi," Bailey explained.

"Well, come home. You know you're not supposed to go anywhere but your grandparents' without permission," her mother told her.

"I have to go," Bailey announced. "Have fun," she forced herself to add. Tears stung her eyes as she headed to the door. She blinked them away. There was nothing to cry about. Her friends were still her friends.

Even though they were avoiding her.

"Sorry, Mom," Bailey said as soon as she stepped into the house. "I just really wanted to see Olivia, and I thought I could catch her on her way out of karate."

"Next time, ask first," her mother said.

"I will."

Bailey thought about trying something else on her list of how to cheer up after a hard day, but her day had been so hard, she was sure nothing would help. Then she heard the yips, yaps, and woofs that meant Gus was nearby with his pack of hellhounds.

"Is it okay if I go meet up with Gus?" Bailey asked. When it looked like her mother was about to say no, Bailey quickly added, "We'll be right in the neighborhood."

"Okay," her mother said. "Be back for dinner."

"I will, probably with Gus," Bailey promised, then hurried back outside. She really needed to be with a friend right now. She didn't care if Gus spent the whole time talking about monster movies and telling fart jokes.

She quickly tracked him down. He was standing in front of the Averys' house. They were the ones who had Hans and Franz. George was probably trying to go pick up the wiener dogs, but it seemed like Bruce was having some kind of sit-down strike. When the massive Saint Bernard decided he didn't want to move, everybody had to wait.

"Hey!" she called over the dogs' enthusiastic greetings.

"You can walk one dog. One," Gus told her. He handed her Ginger's leash. The reddish dog was the most obedient one in the pack. Then he stared at Bailey. "What's wrong with you? You look like you're about to puke."

It was like the question smashed a wall inside her and all these words came spilling out. "None of my friends want to hang out with me even Oh because wherever I go Hannah goes and they all think she's so annoying because she copies me all the time and it's like she's tofu and I don't know what to do because Hannah's my cousin and I know it's a hard time for her but now she's making me as crazy as everyone else and—"

Gus held out his hand like a crossing guard stopping traffic. "I thought you just ate a bad hot dog or something. You can't talk about this—"

"I have to talk about it and I know you hate stupid girly drama but all my other friends are involved in the stupid girly drama which isn't stupid by the way it's my life and so you have to let me talk about it because—"

"Hannah, Bailey's coming with us!" Gus yelled.

What? Hannah?

"Great!" Hannah called back. She was crossing the Averys' front lawn with Hans and Franz. The volume of the dogs' barking went up, and Ginger flopped down onto her back as soon as Hannah joined them. "You want belly scratchies, huh?" Hannah asked.

She dropped to her knees on the sidewalk. Hans and Franz immediately started competing to see who could lick her face the most times, while Bruce dripped drool on the top of her head.

Franz got jealous as Hannah started scratching Ginger, and he gave one of Ginger's back paws a little nip. "*Shhhpt!*" The shushing sound Hannah made got Franz's attention. She pointed at him. "None of that," she told him, her voice low and calm. And Franz obeyed!

Bailey looked between her cousin and Gus. It felt like someone was working on her brain with a curling iron. She could hardly form a thought. Gus and Hannah were, what, friends now? She thought they'd only seen each other that one night at the party. "So do you guys do this a lot?" she managed to ask. "Walk the dogs together?"

"She's helped me out a few times. And she went to the shelter with me a couple days ago. Turns out Hannah's like the dog whisperer," Gus told her.

"Actually, I think positive reinforcement is better than some of the Dog Whisperer's methods. I mean, he gets amazing results, but I think a few treats can make dogs learn almost as fast," Hannah answered. It was like being around the dogs had flipped a switch in her, making her relaxed, without the need to look at Bailey before she opened her mouth.

"I'm with you," Gus said to Hannah. "I always have

a pocketful of treats." He glanced at the beagle near the front of his group. "I'm going to have problems with him if I don't get moving."

"I, uh, I should get home. I told my mom I'd only be out for a couple minutes," Bailey mumbled.

"We'll walk that way and drop you off," Gus volunteered.

"Yeah! Let us walk you," Hannah said eagerly.

"No, it's okay. I've got to go."

If she stood there one more second, she'd start crying. She'd really, really needed to talk to a friend. But Hannah had taken over Gus, the way she'd taken over everything.

She hadn't just ruined Olivia's birthday, she was ruining Bailey's whole life!

CHAPTER 11

How to Start a Fantastic Club

. . .

1. Come up with an idea that a lot of people are interested in.
2. Find a teacher sponsor who kids like.
3. Get publicity so everyone who might be interested knows about the club.
4. Ask potential members what they'd like the club to do.
5. Get a couple people to help you organize everything.
6. Find a business to sponsor you.

Bailey needed a list for how to sleep when you were too upset to fall asleep. That was definitely her problem tonight.

Olivia had called after dinner to apologize again for not telling Bailey that she and the others were meeting up at Gianni's. Bailey said she understood. She did. Hannah was her cousin. Bailey was stuck with her. That didn't mean her friends should have to be stuck with her too.

She had the opposite problem with Gus. He liked Hannah too much! She couldn't believe the two of them had been hanging out without either of them even mentioning it to her. How was she supposed to talk to him about all her Hannah problems now that Hannah was suddenly his favorite gal pal?

Bailey knew Gus had tons of friends at his school. But he was still *hers*. It was her house he walked into without knocking. Her house where he showed up for dinner without being invited. They'd taken baths together when they were babies! She shouldn't have to share Gus with Hannah.

Except you're the one who introduced them, a little voice whispered in her head.

Bailey groaned and flopped over onto her stomach, pulling the pillow over her head, as if that would shut up the horrible little voice. It didn't. *You did even more than that*, it continued. *You pushed them together, making them bring the food down to the party. It's not fair to be mad at either of them for being friends.*

She rolled over onto her back. It didn't help. She

got up and headed over to her desk. She flipped open the notebook where she made her lists. Making a list always made her feel more relaxed. But she couldn't think of a list she needed.

Then inspiration hit her. *How My Life Would Be Better If Hannah Wasn't Here* she wrote. She knew it wasn't nice, but the list was just for her. She hadn't been able to vent to her friends, but she could vent on paper. She wrote the number one, and her hand began to fly across the page.

A knock pulled her out of her thoughts. She grinned when she heard two more quick knocks, followed by a pause and two slow ones. It was her and Gus's secret signal. She rushed over to the window and pulled it open. "Hi."

"Hey," Gus answered, jamming his hands into the kangaroo pouch of his sweatshirt. "I wanted to see if you were still in the middle of a meltdown."

She sighed. "I think I'm completely melted." It wasn't really true, but it wasn't like she could tell him how much she wished Hannah would just go back where she came from.

Gus shuffled his feet. "Okay, so what was the deal? Olivia doesn't want to hang out with you because she's afraid you'll bring Hannah?"

"Not just Olivia—Tess and Vivi too!" Bailey burst out, since he'd asked. "Don't tell Hannah."

Gus snorted. "Yeah, I was planning to text her as soon as I got home to say everybody hates her."

"Not hates her," Bailey said, feeling a little stab of guilt. "She's just annoying some . . . a lot . . . of the time."

"She seems okay to me. She's great with the dogs, and everybody at the shelter likes her," Gus answered. "You should hear what she says about you. She's always going on about how great you are, how nice you are to her. She says it's been so much easier starting a new school because of you."

The little stab of guilt turned into a big one. Bailey tried to ignore it. "Yeah, well it's costing me all my friends."

"There's still me," Gus told her.

But only when you aren't with Hannah, Bailey thought.

"Guess what? I made myself a list like the ones you do," Hannah told Bailey two days later in homeroom.

Bailey was glad Hannah hadn't mentioned that when they'd walked to school with Olivia that morning. Olivia had a Bailey-style list going too—a list of the ways Hannah was taking over Bailey's life.

"What's the list for?" Bailey asked, trying to sound interested, trying to *be* interested. After she'd talked to Gus, she'd thought about how hard Hannah's life was right now. Bailey felt like her life was falling apart, but it was Hannah's parents who were getting a divorce, Hannah who was at a new school in a new town.

"You'll see in a few minutes," Hannah answered.

Maybe Bailey could talk to Hannah about some of the things her friends—and, yes, Bailey herself—found annoying. She'd have to be really careful how she said it. She didn't want to hurt Hannah's feelings.

Ms. Brower, their homeroom teacher, walked into the class. Hannah pulled a list out of her backpack and gave it a little wave in Bailey's direction before smoothing it out on her desk.

As soon as Ms. Brower finished calling roll, Hannah raised her hand. "I'd like to know the rules for starting a club at school. Our website didn't give all the details."

Bailey stared at her cousin. *Hannah* wanted to start a club? How had that happened? Bailey hadn't said anything about wanting to start one.

"First, there's a form you'd have to fill out for Principal Lopez, and if she approves it, you'd have to show that there are enough students who'd want to join. You'd have to have a minimum of five to start.

And you'd need to find a teacher or administrator to sponsor your group." Ms. Brower smiled. "What kind of club are you wanting to start, Hannah?"

Hannah glanced down at her list. "A club that supports the animal shelter on Moss Street. One idea I had was that the club could start a program where walking the dogs would be a possible choice for P.E. The dogs don't get enough exercise, and that can lead to behavior problems, which makes it harder to find people who want to adopt them."

Her voice was a little higher than usual, and she sounded a little breathless, but Bailey thought she'd done great.

Penelope, the girl who was the best actress in drama class, raised her hand. "I'd want to join a group like that. I think it's an amazing idea," she said when Ms. Brower nodded at her. "We got my dog from that shelter." Penelope smiled at Hannah.

"I'd join too," said a boy named Taylor, who Bailey didn't really know, without bothering to raise his hand.

"Walking dogs for P.E. I'd love that!" someone else cried.

"Interesting idea," Ms. Brower said. She opened her desk, rifled through a file, then removed a sheet of paper and gave it to Hannah. "I have an idea or two about sponsors, if you get that far. Let me look into it."

Bailey couldn't stop staring at Hannah. She was still having trouble accepting that it was her cousin who'd brought up the idea.

As soon as Bailey got to the cafeteria that day, she rushed to the usual table. Hannah was already there— the first one—and Bailey couldn't wait to talk to her. They hadn't had time between any of their classes.

"Hannah! I love the idea for the club!" Bailey exclaimed. She did love it. She also loved the fact that if her cousin got her club going, Bailey would have time to spend with her friends without Hannah.

"Did I sound nervous when I asked Ms. Brower about it? I was really nervous," Hannah said.

"Hardly at all. Drama class is paying off," Bailey answered.

"True. I'm getting more used to talking in front of people because of drama," Hannah agreed. "I never would have taken it if it wasn't for you. And I definitely would have fainted during that first exercise, the one where we had to be aliens, if you weren't right there with me. You've been great. I was just telling Gus how great you've been. You've helped me meet so many people. That really helped this morning too. I was talking to people I already know. I've never felt like this at a school."

Bailey felt a mix of pride and guilt. "What are cousins for?" she asked. "Okay, now, the first thing you've got to do, after you find a sponsor, is to get a few people to be a sort of committee to get the club up and running. Then—"

"I've got it covered," Hannah told her as Tess slid into the next seat. "Like I said, I did what you always do. I made a list. Gus helped. He said I should make sure to explain how getting dogs more exercise would make it easier to find them homes. I knew exercise improved their behavior, but I hadn't really thought about it that way."

"Gus helped," Bailey repeated, feeling ashamed that the idea stung. Gus wasn't her personal property. And it really was going to be great to have some time when Hannah was busy with something of her own.

"Yeah," Hannah answered. "We got to talking about dogs at your party. And then I started helping him with the walking, and after I went to the shelter with him one day, I couldn't stop thinking about all the dogs there that needed homes. Then I got the idea. He said

I should go for it."

"I already heard about the idea for the club. It's rad," Tess told Hannah. "I hate watching those commercials on TV with all those sad dogs in cages."

"Maybe Tess could be one of your coorganizers," Bailey suggested. She smiled. Just the possibility of the club had made Hannah stop repeating everything Bailey said. Maybe the Hannah problem would go away now.

"I'd be into that," Tess answered. "Maybe you could start a cat club, Bailey. You're more of a cat girl. I bet Kitty City would love that. Although cats don't need to be walked. You could collect old newspaper for the litter boxes or something." She turned back to Hannah. "I have a dog that is so completely bad. He's almost three, and he still chews up everything. Would walking him more help, do you think?"

Hannah launched into an explanation of the best way to stop a dog from chewing. Bailey didn't have anything she could add. "I'm going to go buy a drink," she mumbled, then hurried away. The two of them clearly wouldn't miss her!

When she returned to the table with a lemonade, Vivi and Olivia were there. So was a teacher she didn't know. "If you want me to, I can read over the application before you turn it in to Principal Lopez," he said to Hannah. "I talked to her for a few minutes, and I know she thinks a club like yours could be great for the school."

"Hannah already has a sponsor, and pretty much guaranteed approval from the principal. Isn't that amazing?" Tess asked after the teacher walked away. "It turns out Mr. Kelly is an extreme dog lover."

"That was so fast," Vivi commented. She started a little cartoon of Hannah in front of a group of kids and dogs. Clearly, Hannah leading the club. "He sounded really excited about it too."

"Ms. Brower must have been," Hannah said. "Since she already told him about it."

"Coolocity," Olivia commented. "It's a fantastic idea. I for one would much rather walk a dog than play volleyball. Karate is the only sport where I don't constantly injure myself."

"I'm not sure dog walking would be safe for you," Bailey told her friend. "Some of them pull hard. And knowing you, you'd end up tangled in the leash and dragged down the street."

"I'd make sure to get a purse dog," Olivia said.

Didn't Olivia get that this was Hannah's club? Why would she want to be in a club with a person who made her crazy? And why hadn't she realized that if Hannah was busy with a club, Olivia and Bailey would actually be able to hang out by themselves sometimes?

"Here she is." Penelope ushered a girl who was at least in seventh grade, and maybe eighth, over to the table. "Hannah, this is my big sister, Ash. She's one of the people who works on the school blog. She wants to write about you and the dog club."

"I think my cousin's idea is great," Bailey said, but Ash didn't even look at her.

"We're only starting to figure the club out," Hannah told Ash. "We don't have permission to start it yet." Then Hannah met Ash's gaze and smiled. "I think I already have a sponsor, though."

"Penelope told me you were only beginning to plan. But I think it would be cool to cover the whole process of starting a school club," Ash explained. "It'll also be a great way to let people who could be interested in the club know what's going on. If you do get the club up and running, I'll be joining."

"I'd definitely join too," Penelope said.

"So can we find someplace a little quieter to talk?" Ash asked Hannah. "I want to get some background on you. And if I can find Clay, I want him to get your picture. He's the blog photographer. He's the best."

"Will you watch my stuff?" Hannah asked Bailey.

"Sure," Bailey said.

It took her a few moments after her cousin walked away to realize she was sitting at a table with Olivia, Vivi, and Tess. Alone! No Hannah.

"Vivi, what's up with your brother? Is he still hogging the bathroom and leaving zit poppage all over the mirror?" Bailey asked, eager to catch up with her friends.

"Penelope's sister isn't just a writer for the school blog," Vivi said. "She's eighth-grade vice president. Hannah's running with the big dogs." She laughed. "Big dogs. I didn't even think about it the other way."

Olivia looked over at Bailey and smiled. "I guess Hannah's finally feeling really settled in at school, since she's starting a club. She'll make tons of new friends now. She was getting on my nerves, but I'm glad we helped her out."

"I have to remember to ask Hannah how to stop Pepper from digging. He's always escaping under the fence. We should have named him Houdini," Tess commented. "That might be a good thing to talk about at a club meeting. Maybe we could also train the dogs instead of just walking them." She winked at Bailey. "I think I'll be like you and start making a list." Tess took out a notebook and pen and started to write.

"Maybe I could do some flyers for Hannah," Vivi said. "Dogs are one of my favorite things to draw."

Finally they had some time alone without Hannah—and all they were going to talk about was Hannah? That was so wrong.

CHAPTER 12

How to Be Chosen
Sixth-Grade Spirit Week MVP

• • •

1. Host practice sessions for challenges.
2. Bring extra supplies—like for costumes—to school in case people forget.
3. Cheer for your class at every event.
4. Wear school colors on days when there aren't costumes.
5. Send text reminders to everyone of what the next day's events will be.
6. Be a star!
7. Relax!!!

"What a pair," Bailey murmured to herself. That was the costume theme for the first day of Spirit Week. It was finally almost here. It started on Monday! Now that Bailey had some Hannah-free time, Bailey could focus on a goal for herself—getting voted sixth-grade MVP. She wanted to win those Katy Perry tickets. Olivia loved Katy Perry. If Bailey won, she'd take Olivia to the concert as a makeup birthday adventure.

First she needed to think of the perfect costume. She tapped her pen against her lip, then wrote down *Candy Crush characters*, then added *pair of dice*.

"What else?" She tapped her lip harder. She didn't know why she always made her lists with a notebook and pen instead of on the computer. Somehow she just got more ideas with a pen in her hand.

Thing One and Thing Two? Maybe that was babyish. It *was* Dr. Seuss. She definitely didn't want to risk looking infantile in middle school! She didn't write it down. Maybe they could both be minions from *Despicable Me*? Or was that babyish too?

Bailey nibbled on the end of her pen. She didn't usually have such a hard time coming up with ideas. Olivia called her an idea machine. Maybe she needed a break. She pulled up the school blog to see if the post on Hannah and the club was on it yet.

Nope. Well, she'd just had that mini-interview a couple of days ago. Bailey refreshed the page, just in case the post had gone up. Nope.

She returned to her list and added *Angry Bird and pig*. Then she got it. Got! It! Elphaba and Glinda from *Wicked*. That was perfect. Bailey didn't even care which one she was—although Hannah would probably let her pick. It would be fun to go all froufrou in pink or to paint her face green.

Bailey grabbed her cell and sent Hannah a text.

perfect costumes for mon. elphaba + glinda.

Impatiently, she waited for Hannah to text back. She had to love the idea. Who wouldn't love the idea?

Bailey refreshed the school blog again—nothing new—then searched for images of the *Wicked* characters. She started a new list of things she and Hannah would need: *broom, wand, tiara, pointed hat—*

Her phone buzzed, and she dropped her pen and grabbed it. Her mouth fell open when she read the text from Hannah.

sorry. tess + me already partners. sorry!!!

no prob, Bailey texted back.

Wow. She'd been sure she and Hannah would be partners. Sometimes it felt like Hannah hadn't been more than two feet away from Bailey since Hannah moved to town. And it wasn't as if the club had gotten actual members yet. It hadn't even really started.

Clearly Tess and Hannah were becoming friends, real friends. And that meant—Bailey and Olivia could be partners! Whoop! She shot off a text to Olivia.

guess what? we can b partners for the costume contest. h + tess teaming.

While she waited for Olivia to answer, she went back to the school blog. Still nothing. She was just so curious what the article would say about Hannah. And how long the post would be. And if there would end up being a picture. And if Hannah would say she was Bailey's cousin.

She hit refresh a couple more times, then texted Olivia again. She was too excited to wait for her to answer.

me + you. glinda + elphaba = awesomness, right???

Olivia answered a few seconds later.

oh nos. thought u + hannah. me + vivi already.

Bailey felt like she'd just swallowed an ice cube— and that the cold, hard lump was jammed halfway down her throat. She couldn't believe Olivia already had a partner. It had only been announced today that the first costume competition would be for teams.

kk, Bailey texted back. BOL!!!

u 2, Olivia answered.

Relax! Bailey ordered herself. *Relax, relax, relax.*

Everybody can't have a partner yet. Her thumbs flew over her cell keys as she sent text after text. After text. After text. After text.

Until she had to accept she was wrong. Everybody she knew *did* already have a partner.

What was she going to do? There's no way she could be Spirit Week Most Valuable Player for her class if she didn't participate in the very first event!

Bailey took a bite of her Cheerios. *Eww. Soggy.* So soggy they almost weren't even *O*s anymore.

"What's wrong?" her father asked, glancing up from the Saturday crossword puzzle for a whole three seconds.

"My cereal's all smushy," Bailey complained.

"Probably because you've been staring at it for the last half an hour instead of eating it," her dad said.

"Really?" It didn't feel like she'd been sitting at the kitchen table that long.

"Really," he told her. "What were you thinking about so hard?" He started to fill in a letter, then hesitated.

"Spirit Week. It starts on Monday," Bailey said. "I want to triumph."

He laughed. "Well, whip up one of your lists. That usually works for you." He brought his pen close to one of the squares but still didn't commit to filling it in.

A list wouldn't help this time. It wasn't like Bailey could make a partner out of paper and ink.

Or wait. Could she? Not with paper and ink, but maybe with cloth, and papier-mâché, and some sparkles, for starters.

"You look like you've just had what your mother—and Oprah, I suppose—would call an aha moment," her dad commented.

"I did!" Bailey exclaimed. Her idea would take a lot of work, though. And she couldn't ask Olivia or any of her friends for help. They were the competition. Well, the seventh and eighth graders were the real competition, but her friends were her competition for sixth-grade MVP, and they probably wanted to win the concert tickets as much as she did.

She took another bite of her cereal and grimaced.

"Get a fresh bowl and leave that for Gus." Her father finally put a letter in one of the boxes of his puzzle. "That kid will eat anything." He looked at the kitchen clock. "Where is he this morning, anyway? He always hits us up for a second breakfast after his post-paper-route nap."

Gus! Gus didn't go to her school. He could help. He wouldn't want to. But she'd done him lots of favors.

And if reminding him of that didn't work, she could also remind him that she had a ton of dirt on him. One way or the other, he'd be helping her.

"Dad, can you take me to the craft store later?" Bailey asked as she dumped her cereal in the sink. She didn't think even Gus would want the mush.

"I think I can work that into my schedule," he said.

"First I have to talk to Gus. Okay if I head over there?"

"If you tell me what Little Jack Horner's last words were," he answered.

"Easy-peasy. He stuck in this thumb, and pulled out a plum, and said—"

"What a good boy am I," Bailey and her dad said together.

"See, you knew it all along," Bailey told him. "Remember to tell Mom where I am. I don't want her to think I left without saying where."

He nodded, and she sped out the door, cut across her lawn, then Gus's, and knocked on his door. "Is Gus around?" she asked when his mother answered.

"He's over at the Speedy Clean car wash. They're letting the animal shelter where he volunteers do a fund-raiser there," Gus's mother answered.

Bailey ran back home, got permission to go downtown, and took off again. She skidded to a stop when she reached the car wash. Gus was covered in suds shaken off by a Great Dane that did *not* want a bath. Hannah was standing next to Gus, holding the dog's leash and laughing as she brushed soap bubbles off her sweatshirt. They looked like they were having a blast.

"Bailey, hi!" Hannah called.

She shouldn't be surprised that Hannah was here. She was all about the shelter now. Bailey headed over but stayed out of the Great Dane's range. "Hi, guys," Bailey answered. "Hey, Gus, when you're done, I need you to help me with something. Your mom has a hot-glue gun, right? Bring that."

"Can't. We're having two more dog washes today, in different parts of town," he told her. Hannah tightened her grip on the Great Dane's leash. It had started to do something that looked like tap dancing in its eagerness to get away from the soap and water. "*Shhpt,*" Hannah said. "Easy, Big Ben." The dog calmed down a little.

"Well, tomorrow then," Bailey said.

Gus shook his head. "It's a whole weekend thing. Tomorrow we're doing a big adoption fair at Frank Liske Park. We're giving baths to all the dogs that are up for adoption too. It's crazy."

It also looked pretty fun. Bailey waited for Gus to ask her to help out. Yeah, she was on Team Cat, but she could handle washing a dog.

He didn't ask. That wasn't usual Gus. Usual Gus would just hand her the shampoo and point at a pup.

It's because he has Hannah to help him, and she's a lot better with dogs than I am. Bailey felt a twinge of jealousy.

She told herself she was being silly. She'd wanted Hannah to make friends. That was why she'd had the party. That was even why she'd told Gus and Hannah to take the food downstairs together. Gus would always be her brother from another mother, no matter how good of friends he got to be with Hannah. She should be happy.

She really should be.

Bailey snarled in frustration. Actually snarled. She just wasn't *crafty*. If Hannah was her partner, they'd be finished already. Hannah could make anything. Bailey used the back of her hand to wipe her sweaty bangs off her forehead, and pink sparkles rained down on the kitchen table. How had they gotten in her hair?

Didn't matter. She had to keep going. It was already

three o'clock. She could maybe convince her parents to let her stay up until ten, even though it was Sunday and she had school in the morning. That only gave her seven hours.

She'd started working on her costume yesterday. She'd already put in—she did a fast calculation—eighteen and a quarter hours. And she wasn't close to being done.

Because she wasn't crafty. Or artsy. She flexed her hand. It was aching from all the cutting she'd been doing. Her fingers felt weird. She snarled again when she realized that she'd managed to. glue two of them together. At least she hadn't been using a hot glue gun, only superglue. Even so, a layer of skin came off as she pried her fingers apart.

"Oh, Bailey. Oh my."

Bailey hadn't even heard her mom come into the room. "It's a disaster. It's the *Titanic* of craft projects."

"It's not that bad. There won't be any casualties," her mother said.

"There already have been." Bailey held up her injured fingers, then moved back her bangs again to show the bruise on her forehead. "I dropped the tiara on the floor, then hit my head on the table when I leaned over to pick it up. I also got a paper cut on my chin.

Don't ask me how." She pointed to the little scratch. "And I stubbed my toe on a box of plaster lawn gnomes at the craft store yesterday."

When she leaned over to rub the toe, which was still sore, she heard a muffled snorting sound. She jerked up her head and saw that her mother had both hands pressed over her mouth as she struggled not to laugh.

"I'm sorry," Mom said. "It's just that you get it from me. Once I was trying to make some felt Christmas tree ornaments. I was leaning over cutting out a felt reindeer, and I ended up giving myself a very bad asymmetrical haircut at the same time. My hair was longer back then."

"Good thing mine is short," Bailey said. She looked at the clock again. "Do you think I could stay up late, just this one time?"

"How late are we talking?" her mother asked.

She needed the whole night, but she knew that she'd never get the okay for that. "Midnight?" she asked.

"Not with school in the morning. Ten at the latest," her mother countered, which was what Bailey had figured she'd say. "You want me to try to help?"

"Thanks. But no." Bailey had learned years ago not to get her mother involved in projects involving glue, scissors, or needles.

"I know! I could call your aunt. She got all the crafty

talent. That's why I have none. She'd help you, I'm sure," Mom said.

Bailey shook her head. "I'm competing against Hannah. I can't ask her mom to help me." She narrowed her eyes at her mother. "You wouldn't help Hannah beat me at something, would you?"

"No way," her mother answered, crossing her heart like a goofball.

"It's not like Hannah needs help anyway," Bailey muttered. "I'm sure she even did Tess's costume for her."

"Show me what you've got so far," her mom said.

Bailey nodded at the bent tiara, wad of white cloth, wad of black cloth, half-empty packet of sparkles, and hunk of black yarn tangled at her feet. She'd decided to go as *both* Glinda and Elphaba—one on the front of her body and one on the back. It had seemed so cool, so perfect, when she'd come up with the idea of being her own partner.

"Maybe you need to try something different," Mom suggested, her eyes wide as she stared at the lump of craft supplies. "This costume might be a little ambitious."

"Starting all over now isn't going to help. Or maybe it would. I don't know." Hopelessness washed over Bailey.

She was going to be out of the running for MVP on day one! And she wanted to go to that concert with Olivia. They really needed a makeup birthday celebration.

She couldn't believe Oh had teamed up with Vivi, although it had made sense that she'd assumed Hannah and Bailey would be partners. Bailey was sure she and Olivia would have found a way to make the Glinda/Elphaba costume awesome, even with Bailey's tendency for what Oh would call craftastrophies and Olivia's own tendency to spill stuff.

"Maybe I should forget it. It would be worse to show up in some hideous falling-apart costume than wear regular clothes," Bailey said. It felt like cement had been added to her blood. Her body was getting heavier and heavier. Just the thought of figuring out a new costume—and then making it—was exhausting.

"Who is this girl sitting in front of me?" her mother asked. "She looks like Bailey, but it can't *be* Bailey. Bailey's a genius at figuring out how to get things done." She planted her hands on her hips. "You're her evil twin, aren't you?"

"Not funny, Mom. I can't—"

Bailey leaped to her feet, a fresh shower of sparkles pinging down on the floor. "Actually, that's perfect!"

"What is?"

Bailey didn't answer. Her mom had just given her inspiration for a new costume. If Bailey could pull it off, it would be perfect! Maybe even a win for the sixth grade!

CHAPTER 13

How to Work a Runway

• • •

1. Confidence, confidence, confidence.
2. Attitude, attitude, attitude.
3. Face, face, face.
4. Posture, posture, posture.
5. Work it all over the place!
6. (Relax!!)!!

Bailey stood in front of the bathroom mirror the next morning, a pair of scissors clenched in her sore fingers. *You can do this,* she told herself. *It's supposed to look messy.* She sucked in a breath, then cut a six-inch chunk of her hair.

Well, not her *hair* hair. The hair of the red wig she'd worn when she went as Merida from *Brave* for Halloween a few years before. She kept snipping until she had it at collar length, then cut some bangs. *Not bad,* she decided.

"Dad, I need you to tie my tie," she called as she stepped into the hall. He'd had one that was pretty close to what she'd needed—maroon with white stripes.

"Looks better on you than it does on me," her dad said when he'd made the knot for her. "The sweater too. Good luck today!"

"Thanks!" Bailey's heart was beating a little faster than usual, and she hadn't even left the house. So much for the relax part of her list. She checked her backpack to make double sure that the copies she'd made were in there. Yep.

She stepped out into the sunlight. "You're going as Chucky?" Gus called from his driveway. "I thought you were supposed to be part of a pair."

If he was too dumb to get who she was, Bailey wasn't going to explain it to him. She hoped no one at school would think she was that doll from that horror movie Gus loved. The only thing that was even a little the same was the red hair.

"Better be careful. I think Chucky went after his next-door neighbor first," Bailey answered. She'd watched one of those movies with Gus once. Mainly because he had said she'd get too scared if she did. She hadn't gotten scared at all.

"No, he didn't," Gus told her. "First he went after the—"

"Got to go to school. Unlike you, I don't have a chauffeur." Bailey turned and waved as she started across her lawn.

"Did you see Hannah's costume? It rocks," Gus yelled after her.

Bailey spun around and strode over to him. "You saw it?"

"Yeah, I helped her and Tess with one little part," he answered.

He helped Hannah? "You said you didn't have time to help me," she accused.

"That's what you wanted the other day?" he said.

"Yeah. And you said no." How could he turn her down and not Hannah? Bailey had known him a million times longer.

"We had some time when we were riding between the different dog washes," Gus explained. "She told me what she was thinking, and it was pretty easy. I brought some stuff to the park on Sunday and worked it out between dogs."

"Well, thanks for nothing," Bailey said, then started away again, not bothering to wave this time.

"You're welcome!" Gus shouted after her.

He was such a pain. Hannah could have him.

Bailey walked to school by herself. Hannah had texted that she was going over to Tess's for a little while before school to finish up their costumes, and Olivia said part of her and Vivi's costume was big, so her mom was driving them.

She hesitated for a moment at the edge of the lawn in front of school. The judges for the costume contest were going to be stationed in the hallway between the principal's office and the cafeteria. Everyone who was entering had to walk down that "runway" before homeroom. The winners would be posted on the bulletin board outside the caf by lunch.

Would they even let her enter? Or would they tell her not to bother since she hadn't followed the rules and didn't have a partner?

Partner or not, she *had* come as a pair. Bailey straightened her shoulders, walked straight to her locker, dumped her stuff, except for the copies she'd made, then walked directly to the end of the runway. There was already a line of kids stretching around the corner.

"Bruce Banner! Hulk! Nice!" she exclaimed when she got in line behind two sixth-grade boys. Encouraging people in her grade was part of her MVP strategy. She would have said it anyway. It was a cool idea.

"What about us?" Bailey heard Olivia call.

Two girls dressed in all green inched out of the line ahead of her and slowly turned around. When they did, Bailey saw they were Oh and Vivi. They had their faces painted green too. Their heads poked through two holes cut in a large peapod, made out of what Bailey thought was plywood covered with some kind of shiny green cloth. Two stuffed pea heads were attached on either side of their faces. They were perfectly sewn, of course.

"Peas in a pod!" Bailey cried. "Excellent! You look amazing!"

"You look—"

Olivia was interrupted by the sound of wheels on linoleum. Bailey turned around and saw Hannah and Tess roller-skating towards the line, hand in hand. Blinking lights flashed in their wheels, and on their jerseys, helmets, and knee pads. The lights had to be Gus's contribution. He was good with electrical stuff.

Tess's jersey said THE PRIM REAPER and Hannah's said THE GLITTERATOR. The names were spelled out in sequins and fake jewels. Hannah's work, for sure. Bailey could hear kids repeating the names and laughing. She forced herself to clap. "Love the eye, Hannah!" she called. One of Hannah's eyes had been covered in black makeup.

"And the teeth, Tess!" Three of Tess's teeth had been blacked out.

She noticed the line moving forward, so she turned around and moved up too. Olivia and Vivi were just turning the corner to start down the runway. Three more teams, then it was Bailey's turn.

Confidence, attitude, face, posture, work it, relax. Confidence, attitude, face, posture, work it, relax. She silently chanted the words until she was up. Then she strode around the corner with what she hoped was a cocky smile on her face. Kids who weren't competing or who had already finished lined both sides of the hall leading to the judges' table.

Bailey turned to the left and handed one of the flyers she'd made to the closest girl. "Fred Weasley. Co-proprietor, Weasleys' Wizard Wheezes. Come by the shop, love," she said in her best British accent. She handed another girl one of the copies. Bailey had created an ad for a blowout sale at the fictional joke shop on the computer.

She took a few steps, then turned to the right. She shook the hand of a boy who had to be in the eighth grade, because that was demonstrating attitude with a capital A. "George Weasley, mate. Come by the shop."

She handed him a flyer, and he grinned at her. Yes, grinned!

She took a few more steps, then turned to the left again. "Fred Weasley, friends. Come to the shop. Why are you worrying about You-Know-Who? You should be worrying about U-No-Poo—the constipation sensation that's gripping the nation?" she called, quoting the sign in front of the Weasleys' shop. It had been in *Harry Potter and the Half-Blood Prince*.

She kept going, being the first part of her pair—Fred—whenever she was facing left, and the second part of her pair—George—when she was facing right. Her mom had given her the idea when she'd pretended she was talking to Bailey's evil twin. Bailey had realized if she dressed as identical twins, she only needed one costume. And the Weasley twins didn't even need sparkles. No glue necessary.

Principal Lopez laughed when Bailey handed her a flyer. Bailey thought that was a good sign. At least she hadn't gotten kicked out of the competition!

Bailey edged closer to the scoreboard outside the cafeteria. Everyone was checking it out before they went in to lunch. She stood on her toes and was able to see who had won first place—a team of seventh graders.

She spotted Penelope right at the front of the crowd. "Did sixth grade win anything, Pen?" she called.

Penelope looked over her shoulder and gave Bailey a thumbs-up. "Your cousin and Tess came in second. That's twenty-five points for our grade! And you! You got a special award—Most Original. That gives us ten more points. So we're in second place."

"Woo!" Bailey cried. She'd contributed ten points by herself. She'd call that valuable!

She gave out the last of her Weasleys' Wizard Wheezes flyers as she walked into the cafeteria for lunch. The tables had been rearranged, leaving a large empty space in the center of the room.

She found Tess and Olivia and sat down. "Hi, there, Most Original," Olivia said with a smile.

Bailey smiled back. "And here's to you, Miss Second Place." She bowed toward Tess, then said, "I wonder what the first challenge will be." Each lunch period during Spirit Week, there would be challenges where the grades could earn points. They weren't announced in advance, so there was no way to prepare.

"If it involves knocking somebody down, I'm ready," Tess answered, slapping one of her knee pads.

"Yeah, I'm sure that's it," Olivia teased. "And the next challenge will be who can stop a wound from spurting blood the fastest."

Bailey cracked up. It felt like it had been forever since she'd laughed with her friends.

Hannah rushed over to the table, Vivi right behind her. "I found out what the challenge is!" she exclaimed. "Josh, this seventh-grade boy who wants to be in my dog club, is on the student council, and he gave me a heads-up. Only a couple minutes heads-up, though. They're going to announce it in a sec."

"Tell us, tell us," Olivia begged.

Hannah knew someone on the student council? Hannah hadn't even been at the school that long! It wasn't really fair. Although Bailey had only been in the school two weeks longer. But she'd lived in town her whole life. Hannah shouldn't know people Bailey didn't know.

That was what you wanted to happen, that little voice, that truly annoying little voice, in Bailey's head whispered. *You wanted her to meet people. You wanted her to make friends. And now you're mad because your plan worked!*

"You know that game Taboo? Where you have to get

your partner to say a word without using a list of other words? Like if you got 'blue' as your word, you wouldn't be able to say things like 'water' or 'sky,'" Hannah said. "It's going to be like that. We're going to compete with our partners from the costume contest."

"I should win then," Bailey joked. "Since my partner happens to share my brain." Then it hit her. She wouldn't be able to compete. Her two-in-one costume idea had worked great, but she couldn't play the game by herself.

"Oh no! You're not going to be able to play!" Hannah cried.

"It's okay. Maybe I can be a timekeeper or something," Bailey answered. That would be a good way to be valuable.

Hannah gave a little frown. "When I was talking to Josh, it sounded like all that was already organized by the student council. They're having teachers and administration do it."

Bailey nodded. "I'll be your cheering section, then." She had to try really hard to smile, but she did it.

If Hannah hadn't moved here, I would be Olivia's partner, she couldn't help thinking. *Oh wouldn't have teamed up with Vivi, because she wouldn't have thought*

I was going to be partners with Hannah.

And Bailey and Olivia would have triumphed at this challenge. They were BFFs. That meant they could pretty much read each other's minds.

CHAPTER 14

How to Be a Good Loser

* * *

1. Smile when someone else wins.
2. Congratulate the winner—still smiling.
3. Listen to the winner describe the feeling of winning—
   still smiling.
4. It's okay to have a tantrum—just not in public.
5. It's okay to cry—just not in public.

"I need a ride to the drugstore," Bailey called when she walked in her front door that afternoon.

"Words like *hello, hi, greetings,*" her father said. The restaurant where he worked was closed on Mondays, so he was home.

"Hello, hi, greetings," Bailey obediently parroted. "Can you drive me to the drugstore, please, *por favor?*—" She tried to think of another way to say please, but couldn't. "And I'm out," she admitted.

"'Would you oblige me, favor me, accommodate me with a ride?'" her father suggested, going into crossword-puzzle mode.

"So would you?" Bailey asked.

"It would be my pleasure," he answered. She trailed him when he went to get his car keys off the hook in the kitchen, then followed him out to the car, walking so close she stepped on the heel of one of his shoes.

"A little impatient, are we?" he asked.

"I guess. I just need some stuff for tomorrow's costume competition," Bailey told him.

"Not a staple gun!" he said in mock horror before he got in the car.

"No, the sixth graders have to dress like babies. The eighth graders have to dress like senior citizens, and the seventh graders are dressing like moms and dads," she explained when she was settled in the seat next to him.

"Poor seventh graders." Her dad gave a fake shudder as he pulled out of the driveway.

"Um, how do you feel about making a contribution to a sixth-grade victory?" Bailey asked when they pulled up in front of the drugstore a few minutes later.

"How much are we talking?" he replied.

"Enough for maybe twenty of those suckers shaped like pacifiers," Bailey said. "We don't get judged on costumes tomorrow, but we get points depending on how many people participate. I wanted to give suckers to people who don't bother to dress up or who forget."

Her dad handed her a twenty. "You can buy however much school spirit this will give you."

"Thanks, blessings—" Bailey thought for a few seconds. "And I'm out again."

"One thanks is plenty," her father said.

Bailey almost skipped into the store. And she almost gave a cheer when she spotted the bag of brightly colored pacifier suckers. How valuable were they going to be tomorrow? Very, extremely, remarkably, exceedingly, greatly, and all the other ones she couldn't think of right now!

Bailey felt like she was walking through a bouncy house when she entered the school the next morning. She was so happy, she felt *springy*. She couldn't wait to start giving out the pacifier suckers.

"I have a surprise," she announced to Olivia and Hannah. She opened her backpack and pulled out the bag of suckers. "These are for anyone who didn't dress up. We're going to rack up the participation points!"

"Brilliant!" Olivia exclaimed. She tightened the ties of her baby bonnet. It kept slipping off her head.

"I brought something too!" Hannah opened her backpack and pulled out a wide, shallow plastic box. She opened it so they could see that the inside was divided into little sections, and each section held pink beads, blue beads, or beads with letters on them. The beads without the letters had tiny rattles and diapers glued on them—more of Hannah's DIY stuff, definitely. "They're to make baby bracelets. I already made some for us, and Tess, and Vivi, and a few other people." She handed one to Bailey and one to Olivia.

"Oh, it's so adorable," Olivia crooned. She held out her wrist. "Tie it on me." Hannah did.

"They're really cute," Bailey said. Her voice came out sounding kind of flat. "What a great idea," she added, because it really was. She held out her wrist so Hannah could tie on her bracelet; then she tied on Hannah's for her.

"I got the idea from you," Hannah said.

"Huh?" Bailey didn't get it.

"Not for the bracelets," Hannah explained. "But to do something for people who didn't dress up. Your mom told my mom about the suckers, so I decided to do something too!"

Bailey couldn't believe her mother had done that. Her suckers were a way for her to get chosen MVP. But now that Hannah had brought something for the class too, they weren't special anymore.

If she was truthful, Hannah's bracelets were cooler than her suckers. Bailey knew for sure every girl was going to want one.

"Between the two of you, we're going to triumph." Olivia gave a little clap. "We'll *have* to get more participation points than the other grades."

Bailey managed to smile. That was the whole point. She'd wanted to help her class win. And at least her costume was better than Hannah's—not that they were getting points for best costume today, only points for each person who dressed up. Hannah had on a pale blue T-shirt with a yellow ducky appliqued on it. Bailey had borrowed her mom's baby-doll pajamas. They were too big, but she'd pinned the waist of the adorable little bloomers with the tiny ruffles on the legs, and it didn't matter that the top was oversized.

"Maddy!" Hannah called to one of her classmates. "You need to be wearing something baby for the competition."

"I know!" she answered. "I had dance last night, and my mom said it was too late to go find something after."

"Not a problem," Hannah said. "I'll make you a bracelet."

"Can you hold this?" Hannah held the plastic box out to Bailey without waiting for her to answer, then started picking the beads she needed to spell Maddy's name. Bailey hadn't even had the chance to offer a sucker.

Ash wandered over. "I love those bracelets." She fingered the one on Hannah's wrist. "Will you make one for me?"

"Sorry. Sixth graders only," Hannah said with a smile.

Ash gave an exaggerated pout, then smiled back. "We need some people like you in my grade."

"Hey, Brian! You need something baby. Take one of these." Olivia waved a boy in their grade over. She took one of the pacifiers out of the bag and tossed it to him.

"Nice." He unwrapped it and popped it into his mouth as he wandered off.

Bailey hadn't been able to give it to him herself because she was holding Hannah's stupid box. And Olivia hadn't bothered to tell Brian that the sucker was from her. It wasn't fair.

Don't be a baby, she told herself, as Penelope dragged a boy over and asked for bracelets for both of them.

Bailey gave a fist pump when she checked out the scoreboard at lunch. The sixth grade had gotten fifty points because they'd had the most people participate in the costume contest. She knew that win was partly due to her. And Hannah.

The important thing was that Bailey had helped. Yeah, it would be cool to be chosen MVP, and she still wanted that. But having the sixth grade win the whole Spirit Week competition—that would be awesome.

"I found out what the contest is going to be today, thanks to my student council source," Hannah said when Bailey joined her friends at their lunch table.

"I love getting the inside scoop," Olivia said. "You're the man, Hannah."

"I'm so the man," Hannah agreed with a laugh, something she never would have said when she first got to town. She really had gotten comfortable at the school and with Bailey's friends.

We're only getting the info a few minutes early, Bailey thought. *It's not like she found out last night.* She shoved the thought away. Things with Hannah were getting better. They really were. For starters, she no longer felt like she was hanging out with a demented parrot. Hannah didn't just repeat Bailey's opinions anymore. And she was making new friends, the way

Bailey had hoped she would.

"It's Name That Tune," Hannah told them.

Vivi groaned. "I'm gonna be so horrible at that."

It was kind of true. Tess always got the names of books and movies and songs a little off. Like instead of *World War Z*, she would say *World Warz*.

"They're only going to have two people from each class play this time," Hannah said.

"That's a relief. I wouldn't want to ruin it for our grade," Vivi answered.

"How're they choosing?" Bailey asked.

Hannah shrugged. "I'm not sure."

The principal stepped out into the middle of the room. When she announced the game, she got big cheers. Bailey bet everyone was going to want to play!

"Raise your hand if you want to represent your class," Principal Lopez told them. Bailey thrust her hand into the air, along with almost everyone in the cafeteria. Bailey was amazed at how many sixth grade kids were wearing the baby bracelets.

"Hannah should be one of ours," a girl Bailey didn't know called out. She had one of Hannah's bracelets on her wrist.

"Yeah, Hannah!" Penelope agreed. "We won the costume challenge today because of her."

"And Daniel," someone else yelled. "He knows every song ever."

"Daniel, Daniel, Daniel!" a couple of kids began to chant.

When Hannah and Daniel stepped into the center of the room, everybody in the sixth grade cheered. Bailey made sure to cheer louder than anyone, even though it was so disappointing not to be able to play for the second day in a row!

Daniel might have known every song ever, but he didn't get the chance to prove it. Neither did the seventh or eighth graders. Hannah was fast on the buzzer. She beat the other kids all but a few times. And out of all the songs she gave titles for, she only got one wrong.

A different chant started up, slowly at first, then faster and faster, louder and louder. Instead of "Daniel, Daniel, Daniel," it was "Hannah, Hannah, Hannah!"

"I still can't believe how awesome Hannah was," Olivia said when she met up with Bailey at her locker after school. "The sixth grade won the day because of her."

"Well, I brought those pacifiers," Bailey muttered.

"Oh, right! That definitely helped too," Olivia answered.

Helped *too*? Hannah wouldn't even have had the

idea to bring something for kids who didn't wear costumes if it wasn't for Bailey. And Bailey's mom blabbing to Aunt Caitlin.

"Maybe I should bring something for tomorrow," Olivia said. "It's Summer Day. I could bring life jackets from the boat. And I bet we have extra pairs of sunglasses."

"That would be great." It's not like she could say that Olivia was stealing Bailey's idea—just like Hannah had. "You should bring your blow-up sea horse," Bailey suggested, reminding herself again that, really, the most important thing was for her grade to win, not for her to be voted MVP.

"I should!" Olivia exclaimed. "I definitely will."

"I'll text you a reminder," Bailey said.

"Thanks, Bails," Olivia answered. "So off to Emmy's, right? We have some celebrating to do. I already told Hannah."

"What?"

"Hannah winning the lunch competition is definitely Emmy's worthy," Olivia said. "Italian sodas all around."

Bailey felt as if Olivia had just slapped her. Celebrations at Emmy's were *their* thing. Just theirs. It wasn't even something they did with Tess and Vivi.

"I'm not sure I can," Bailey answered. What she

really didn't think she could do was sit at Emmy's with Olivia and Hannah. How could Olivia think it was okay? She'd even asked Hannah without checking with Bailey.

"Well, ask," Olivia urged.

Bailey sent her mom a quick text and got a yes back. She decided that was a good thing. It was going to be bad enough to have Hannah glomming on to something that was supposed to be a Bailey-and-Olivia best-friend thing. But it would be even worse to be sitting at home, knowing that Hannah and Bailey were drinking celebratory Italian sodas at Emmy's without her.

"You ready to leave?" Hannah called as she headed down the hall towards them.

"Uh-huh. Congratulations again," Bailey forced herself to say. It was the right thing to do.

"You're going to love Emmy's," Olivia told her as they walked towards the exit. "They have about a million flavors of soda. Raspberry, blueberry, watermelon."

Hannah crinkled up her nose. "Do they have any flavors that aren't fruit? I don't really like fruit drinks."

"You said you loved the watermelon lemonade I made on the day you first got here!" Bailey protested. They stepped outside and started for downtown.

Hannah blushed. "I liked that you made it for me,"

she told Bailey. "Really."

She was so fake. Such a liar. Why did Olivia want to hang around with her?

"No worries," Olivia answered. "They have vanilla bean, and hazelnut, oooh, and butterscotch. I think I'm going to try that one today."

"Seriously?" Bailey couldn't help bursting out.

Bailey always had blueberry and Hannah always had raspberry at their celebrations. Always.

"Yeah, I love blueberry, but I thought it would be fun to try something new. Butterscotch on sundaes is yummy, so it should be yummy to drink," Olivia answered.

"Whatever," Bailey mumbled under her breath, giving a shrug.

"I can't believe you knew that Bad Rabbits song in the competition, Hannah. I've never even heard of them. They were picking some really hard ones at the end," Olivia said.

"It's cause my dad was stationed near Boston for a while, and the Bad Rabbits are from there," Hannah answered. "They're great. They combine all these different styles. I'll send you links to some downloads if you want."

"I want!" Olivia answered. "Have you heard the

Avett Brothers? They're from Concord. They do a great mix of stuff—indie, country, pop, rock, everything." She pulled out her iPhone. "You've got to hear this one." She stuck one of the earbuds in her ear and handed the other one to Hannah.

Bailey listened hard. She was able to make out the song. It was "Living of Love." Olivia hadn't even *heard* of it until Bailey played it for her. Olivia hadn't even heard of the Avett Brothers until Bailey came back from a concert with her dad and told her about them. Now Olivia was acting like she had discovered them, so she could impress Hannah!

Hannah and Olivia didn't take the earbuds out until they got to Emmy's, which was so completely rude. Bailey didn't feel like talking to either of them by the time they sat down at their table.

"Blueberry and raspberry, right?" Suzette, their waitress, wearing her usual cap with the cat ears on it, asked.

"I'm actually switching it up. I'm having butterscotch today," Olivia announced.

"Feeling adventurous, hmmm?" Suzette asked. "What about you, Bailey?" she added.

"Same as always for me. I'm loyal," she said, shooting a hard look at Olivia. Olivia didn't seem to notice.

"And who's this new person?" Suzette asked.

"Hannah Sullivan," Hannah told her. "I moved here a few weeks ago."

Bailey noticed Hannah hadn't bothered to say she was Bailey's cousin.

"So what are we celebrating today?" Suzette smiled. She didn't seem to think it was weird that there was this new person at the table, when celebrating at Emmy's was a Bailey-and-Olivia tradition. Had been for years. Just the two of them.

"Hannah won the Spirit Week competition today." Olivia wrapped her arm around Hannah's shoulder. "The sixth grade is going to decimate the older kids, thanks to my friend here."

CHAPTER 15

How Not to Be Jealous

• • •

1. Think about your own good qualities.
2. Make a list of things you're grateful for.
3. Don't compare yourself to other people.
4. Don't assume you know what people are thinking (like that Olivia likes Hannah more than you).
5. Even if you feel jealous, act like you don't feel jealous.

Bailey studied herself in the mirror, then gave a nod of satisfaction. She definitely looked beachy. She had a pair of hot-pink floaties on her arms and matching bright-pink zinc oxide on her nose. A huge straw hat was on her head, and a huge pair of sunglasses covered her eyes. She wore her dad's ugliest Hawaiian shirt. It had not one, but four, truly ugly patterns on it. With the plastic lei on top, it was hideous. She loved it!

She wasn't going to let Hannah ruin Spirit Week for her. *Okay, not Hannah,* Bailey forced herself to admit as she started the walk to school. Her jealousy of Hannah. It wasn't as if Hannah had done anything wrong by winning the contest yesterday. Bailey *wanted* the sixth grade to win.

And Olivia—well, Olivia was being nice inviting Hannah to Emmy's. Bailey just wished Olivia had chosen a different place. She didn't understand why Olivia didn't understand that Italian sodas at Emmy's was their special thing. She should. It wasn't like they'd ever invited anyone to come along before.

Bailey pushed the thoughts aside. She was going to have fun today, and being mad at Olivia and jealous of Hannah was absolutely not fun. Hannah wasn't waiting on the sidewalk when Bailey got there, the way she usually was, so Bailey went up and knocked on the door.

Her grandmother laughed when she opened it. "Bailey! You look fabulous. The way your nose matches your floaties—it's perfection."

Bailey smiled. She'd missed her grandmother. She hadn't been coming over to visit as much because she hadn't wanted any more Hannah time. That wasn't Hannah's fault either. That had been Bailey's decision.

Impulsively, she wrapped her arms around her grandma and hugged her tight. "It's good to see you."

"You too, sweetie." Her grandmother had to push the brim of Bailey's huge hat away from her face so she could speak.

Her grandfather appeared behind her grandmother. "I'll be chauffeuring you today," he announced.

"Hannah's costume is a little hard to walk in," Grandma explained.

"We have to pick up Olivia too then. She'll be waiting for us," Bailey answered.

"Of course, Olivia too," Granddad told her. "Where there's Bailey, there's Olivia."

Bailey smiled. Everybody knew Olivia was her best friend. That hadn't changed just because Olivia had gotten all involved in that conversation about music with Hannah, or because Oh had invited Hannah to Emmy's. Or even because Olivia had called Hannah her friend. Olivia and Bailey both had lots of friends. That didn't mean they weren't best friends.

"Here she is." Grandma turned and smiled at Hannah.

Bailey's chest went tight. It felt like someone was squeezing her ribs together. Hannah was dressed as a mermaid, totally glamorous in a long emerald-green dress with seashells glued to the hem. Bailey recognized the dress. She'd never seen her grandmother wear it in person, but there was a glam picture of Grandma wearing it when she was in her twenties. Bailey loved that picture. It felt wrong to see that dress on Hannah.

And the seashells! She was almost positive they were from her grandfather's collection. He gathered shells every time he went on vacation near a beach.

Even if you feel jealous, act like you don't feel jealous, Bailey coached herself. "You look awesome, Hannah," she told her cousin.

"Thanks. You too. Your outfit is hilarious," Hannah answered.

Hilarious is what Bailey had been going for, but now she just felt . . . ugly. As ugly as her father's ugly Hawaiian shirt.

"Let's get you two to school," Grandpa said.

"And Olivia," Hannah reminded him.

"Of course Olivia. How could I forget Olivia when she's such a good friend to both my granddaughters?" he answered.

Hannah hardly knows Olivia, Bailey thought. But she didn't say the words aloud.

"Did Hannah tell you I'm getting close to finishing the mural?" Granddad asked after they all got in the car. "The meadow idea really inspired me."

My meadow idea. My meadow, Bailey thought sourly.

"It's going to be amazing!" Hannah exclaimed. "Granddad and I came up with a way to make some of it 3D."

"That was all you," he told Hannah.

"Too bad you won't get to see it much," Bailey blurted out. Hannah and Granddad stared at her. "I mean, aren't you and your mom going to be getting your own place soon?"

"We decided to stay until school's out, then see," Hannah answered.

"Your grandma and I convinced them," Grandpa said. "It's been too long since we've spent any time together."

"Yeah, of course, that's great." Bailey was glad she had on her big dark glasses. That way Grandpa and Hannah couldn't see the tears that had appeared in Bailey's eyes. She had no reason to feel like crying. Of course her grandparents were happy to have Aunt Caitlin and Hannah living with them. They got to be with Bailey and her parents all the time. She was sure they missed their daughter and granddaughter.

"That's really great," Bailey repeated, trying to act like she wasn't jealous. Or hurt.

"Today's competition is called Pretty Kitty!" Mr. Paulson, one of the gym teachers, announced. "We'll do a round with each grade, then the winners from each grade will compete for Spirit Week points. Sixth graders first. If you want to play, sit in a circle over here." He gestured to the open space in the middle of the cafeteria.

Bailey, Olivia, Tess, Vivi, and Hannah all got in the circle, along with about twenty other kids.

"Okay, here's how it works. I'm going to choose someone to be the pretty kitty. The kitty will go up to someone in the circle and that person has to say "pretty kitty" three times—without laughing. If you laugh, you're out. If you don't laugh, the kitty is out, and I pick a new one. Got it?"

After he got a bunch of nods and yeses, Mr. Paulson walked around the circle and tapped Alan, who Bailey had known since kindergarten. "You're up."

Alan got on all fours and crawled toward Samantha, who'd also gone to their elementary school. Good choice. Samantha was a giggler. She didn't get out even one pretty kitty. She was laughing before Alan got all the way over to her. Mr. Paulson jerked his thumb back in a you're-out gesture, and Samantha left the circle, still laughing.

Alan crawled over to Allison next. Another good choice. Allison only managed the "pre" of *pretty kitty*. When Alan shifted around and started toward Bailey, she knew he was out. The last thing she felt like doing today was laughing.

"Pretty kitty, pretty kitty, pretty kitty," she said calmly. And Alan was out.

I've got this, Bailey thought.

She got a little worried when Olivia was picked as the kitty a few rounds later. Oh could always crack her up. She expected Olivia to try her first, but Olivia went to Hannah instead. As soon as Hannah looked at Olivia, she started squeaking with suppressed giggles. Her face turned red, then she let out a huge bray of a laugh. Olivia started laughing too.

Mr. Paulson gave Hannah the out thumb. Neither Hannah nor Olivia noticed. They were laughing too hard. Laughing like they'd forgotten they were in the middle of a game and everyone was waiting for them. Laughing like they had a huge inside joke. Laughing like they were best, best friends.

"Hannah, you're out!" Mr. Paulson had to say it twice before Hannah and Olivia got control of themselves.

Hannah left the circle, and Olivia crawled over to Bailey next. After seeing Olivia and Hannah cracking up together like they'd been friends for a million years, it was easy for Bailey to stay serious.

Even when Olivia rubbed her head against Bailey's knee and gave loud purrs, Bailey didn't feel like smiling. "Pretty kitty, pretty kitty, pretty kitty," she said. Her tone came out sharper than she'd meant it to. Oh well. Everyone would think it was because she was trying so hard not to laugh.

Even when she won the game, she didn't feel like smiling.

Even when she won against the seventh and eighth grade winners, she didn't feel like smiling. She did smile, though. She was good at acting, and that included acting as if it didn't feel like her world was falling apart.

"You feel like making your extreme mac and cheese?" Bailey's mom asked that evening. "Hannah's coming over. She's going to have dinner and spend the night. Your grandfather's been painting her room, and the fumes are too potent for her to sleep in there."

If Bailey was acting as if she wasn't jealous—and as if the world didn't feel like it was falling apart—she would say yes. So she said yes.

She continued her performance all through dinner. She joked around with her dad about serving him the "heart attack special," as he called her version of mac and cheese. She even described Hannah's mermaid costume to them, telling them how cool it looked.

"You should have seen Bailey at today's competition," Hannah said when Bailey had finished telling how amazing Hannah had looked in their grandmother's dress. "She won the whole thing. Fifty points for the sixth grade! We're tied with the eighth graders now!"

"What did you have to do, Bailey?" her father asked. When Bailey described the game, her father raised his eyebrows. "I'm impressed. I've seen you and Olivia laugh at absolutely nothing many times."

"Olivia made me laugh just by looking at me!" Hannah exclaimed. "I couldn't help it. Neither of us could."

Bailey couldn't take anymore. She'd been acting all day. "I'm finished. I have a ton of homework. I'm going to go get started," she announced. She hurried into the kitchen with her plate before her parents could say anything.

She got only about fifteen minutes of privacy before Hannah came into her room. Hannah pulled her math book out of her backpack. "Want to do the math homework together?" she asked.

"I finished it already," Bailey answered. Lie. "I think

I'm going to go take a bath." She wasn't ready for more Hannah time yet.

Even though she stayed in the bathtub until she was basically a giant wet prune, she still didn't feel ready to be in the same room with Hannah. She didn't have a choice, though. It wasn't like she could sleep in the tub.

She got out, took her time drying off and putting on her pajamas, then dragged herself down the hall to her room. Hannah glared at her when she stepped inside. It took Bailey a few seconds to realize that her cousin was holding Bailey's polka-dotted notebook in her hand. The notebook Bailey used to make her lists!

"What are you doing with that?" Bailey demanded.

"I needed some paper. When I opened it, I saw—" Hannah swallowed hard, then her eyes narrowed. "You hate me!"

"I don't hate you," Bailey protested, guilt and anger getting her belly churning.

"Oh, right. That's why you made a list of reasons you wish I'd never moved here." Hannah's voice was low but filled with anger.

"I was just—" Bailey began.

"You wish I wasn't here. That's no different than hating me," Hannah interrupted.

And Hannah was right. At that moment, Bailey

really did feel like she hated her cousin. She knew it was wrong, but that was how she felt.

"Did you see the other lists, though?" Bailey forced herself to ask. She couldn't actually admit she hated Hannah. Her parents would go ballistic. Her grandparents would be so disappointed in her. "There were lists about how to make you feel welcome, and how to help you with your parents' divorce. I gave you a party!"

Bailey had worked really hard on that party too. Didn't Hannah know that?

"What about that list about how not to be annoyed by me? Don't try to say I'm not the annoying person your list was about." Hannah threw the notebook at Bailey. It landed at her feet, its cover bent.

"I won't. You *were* the annoying person." Anger won out over the guilt. "Just so incredibly annoying!"

"How? What did I do? I did everything I could to be nice!" Hannah protested.

"Like copying everything I did?" Bailey demanded. "You got yourself put in almost all my classes. Even drama. And you hate drama. And you're really bad at it. And you glommed on to me every time we had an acting exercise to do with a partner. And you bought the same sneakers as me. And the same scarf, practically! And you painted your nails like mine, with the polka dots! And you agreed with every single thing I said. You were always all 'Me too, me too, me too.' It was sickening." She couldn't stop. All her frustration and anger came flooding out. "And you pushed Olivia out of the way because you wanted to sit by me in Spanish Club—and you don't even take Spanish. You told Gus you were like his cousin, and you barely knew him. You got yourself invited along to Olivia's birthday celebration. Why would you think we'd want you there? You're not our friend."

"I thought we were starting to be friends. I didn't know you hated me," Hannah told her. Her face had gone pale, and her eyes were shiny with unshed tears. "Does Olivia really feel that way too?"

"Of course that's what you care about. What Olivia thinks about you. I know you're trying to get her as your best friend. Don't deny it. Well, she was just being nice to you as a favor to me. She and Vivi and Tess had to go sneaking around behind my back so they could have some time away from you. I didn't even get invited because they knew *I'd* have to bring *you* with me! You ruined my life."

"Well, don't worry. I won't anymore. I never even want to see you again." Hannah snatched up her backpack and strode out the door. A few seconds later, Bailey heard the front door slam.

And a few seconds after that, her mother appeared in the doorway. "What happened? Why did Hannah leave?"

"She was homesick, I guess. She said she'd just sleep on the couch," Bailey answered.

Her mother frowned. "I'll just call and make sure she got home all right. I would have driven her. I know it's only a block, but I don't like her out there at night by herself."

Bailey hoped that Hannah would keep their fight to herself. But even if she didn't, at least the Hannah problem was over. She didn't have to worry about Hannah never leaving her alone.

Hannah had said she never wanted to see Bailey again, and that was perfect! Now Bailey could have every bit of her life back.

CHAPTER 16

How to Lose All Your Friends

• • •

1. Have stupid friends.
2. Have a cousin who's a traitor and can't keep her big mouth shut.

"You didn't dress up?" Olivia stared at Bailey when she showed up the next morning so they could walk to school again.

It hadn't even registered right away that Olivia was dressed as Zatanna, a superhero who was part of the Justice League. She wore a black top hat, white gloves, black pants, and a shiny tuxedo jacket that had been part of her dance recital costume last year, before she switched from dance to karate.

Bailey looked down at herself, as if that would make a superhero costume appear. "I forgot. I totally forgot."

She felt weird, like her brain had been injected with novocaine. All numbed out. She'd spent half the night replaying her fight with Hannah, sometimes feeling bad for what she'd said, but more often feeling like Hannah deserved every single word.

"Are you feeling okay?" Olivia pressed her hand on Bailey's forehead.

"Not really," Bailey admitted. "I'm not sick or anything. Just . . . I don't know."

"Come on in. We can find something for you to wear really fast." Olivia tugged Bailey into the house, then down the hall to the kitchen. She opened the junk drawer and handed Bailey a roll of silver duct tape. "Make yourself some boots with this. Cover your shoes and go up to your knees."

"Who am I going as?" Bailey asked.

"I don't know. A brand-new superhero, I guess." Olivia grabbed a roll of foil. She made a square several layers thick. "Hold still for second." She pressed the foil against Bailey's face, smoothing her hands over Bailey's eyelids, nose, and lips. "Okay, back to the boots," she told Bailey.

While Bailey wrapped the duct tape up one leg, Olivia cut the foil square into an oval, then cut out the places where Bailey's eyes had been and added nostril holes. "Where's Hannah?" she asked. "She's not walking with us today?"

"No." Bailey didn't offer an explanation. Instead, she concentrated on making her tape boots.

Olivia made holes at either side of the mask, then threaded a rubber band between the holes, making knots to keep the band in place. "Be right back. Gotta raid the tornado prep supplies."

Bailey had finished making her boots by the time Olivia came back with a silver Mylar emergency blanket. She tied it around Bailey's shoulders, then helped her put on the mask. "There's got to be a superhero who wears all silver, right?"

"There's a Silver Sable, I think," Bailey answered. Sometimes she read comic books when she was hanging out with Gus.

"Well, they aren't judging costumes. It's only participation points again," Olivia said. "And you'll definitely get those. If we aren't late. Let's get going." She led the way back outside. "What's Hannah doing this morning? Why isn't she walking?"

Bailey shrugged. "Not sure," she answered. Could Hannah be standing in front of her house, waiting for Bailey? Bailey hadn't checked. She hadn't wanted to go anywhere near Hannah. And Hannah had said she never wanted to see Bailey again. So she definitely shouldn't be waiting for Bailey to walk to school with her.

With the last-minute costume creating, Bailey didn't make it to homeroom until about three seconds before the bell. Bailey's gaze went immediately to Hannah, then slid away. She hadn't wanted to look at her cousin. She hadn't been able to help herself. It didn't seem like Hannah wanted to look at her either, her or anybody else. She'd had a book open on her desk, with her nose almost touching the pages.

Bailey tried to concentrate on what Ms. Brower was saying, but with novocaine brain—and the distraction of Hannah sitting a few seats over—it was hard.

You're going to be okay, she told herself when the bell rang. She didn't have any classes with Hannah the rest of this morning, and she really didn't think Hannah would try to sit with Bailey and her friends at lunch.

Would she?

Bailey rearranged the books in her locker by height instead of by the order of her classes, then switched them back. She was stalling. She knew it. She wasn't ready to see Hannah yet.

She won't be at the table, Bailey told herself.

But what if she was? What would Bailey say? What would *Hannah* say? Would they pretend nothing had happened? Would they give each other the silent treatment? Would Hannah yell at Bailey?

She kind of deserved it. She *had* said some horrible things to Hannah last night. But Hannah shouldn't have gone snooping in her notebook. If she needed paper, she should have waited and asked for it. It's not like Bailey would ever have *told* Hannah she was annoying or that Bailey didn't want her around. She wasn't mean like that.

And there had been good lists in the notebook too. Like the list for making Hannah feel welcome, and the one on how to make the lunch really special for Hannah and Aunt Caitlin on their first day. Hannah hadn't given Bailey any credit for that.

Bailey slammed her locker. If Hannah was at the table, maybe Bailey would tell her exactly how ungrateful she was!

She spun the dial on her lock, then turned around to start towards the caf. Olivia was coming towards her, Tess and Vivi right behind her. They looked mad.

"What's wrong?" Bailey asked.

"You told Hannah we hated her?" Olivia demanded. "I can't believe you did that!"

"I didn't. I would never say you hated her," Bailey protested. Heat rushed up her neck and into her face.

"You told her we sneaked around behind your back so we could hang out without her," Vivi snapped.

Bailey jerked her chin up. "Are you telling me you didn't? You know you did! You said she was like tofu!" She whirled towards Tess. "And you said she acted sketchy." She turned on Olivia. "And you said she was weird. And I know you weren't happy she had to come with us for your birthday. Are you going to deny that?"

"No, but why would you tell her any of that?" Olivia asked. "That was so mean, Bailey."

"We know Hannah better now," Tess added. "It's not like we'd still do that. She was obviously just really shy and nervous when she started school, and that's why she acted the way she did."

"You really hurt her feelings," Vivi said.

They were all ganging up on her. They weren't even giving her a chance to explain. They were just assuming she'd been mean and horrible on purpose. How could they do that, when they'd been her friends forever?

"I didn't mean to tell her. I really, really didn't," Bailey explained. "Actually, I *didn't* tell her. She went snooping through my stuff and saw some lists I'd made."

"You had something about us getting together without her on one of your lists?" Olivia sounded skeptical.

"Sort of. But it was just for me. It was private," Bailey had to admit. "I can't believe she went and tattled to you about that."

"It wasn't like that," Olivia told her. "In history, I could tell she was really upset. I asked her what was wrong. She wouldn't say at first, but I kept asking and she finally told me. I'm glad she did. That way I could tell her the truth."

"The truth?" Bailey demanded. "You mean that you all found her insanely annoying at first? That you had to plan a secret meeting—without me—because you couldn't stand to be around her?"

"We shouldn't have done that. I already told her I was sorry," Tess said.

"We all did," Olivia told Bailey. "Now you have to too."

"You're supposed to be my best friend, Olivia. But you're acting like you care a lot more about Hannah. It's all about how *she* feels. Don't you even care that she's ruining my life?" Bailey cried.

"I would care if she was," Olivia answered. "She's not, though. She's not copying you anymore. She's not repeating everything you say or agreeing with you all the time. And those are the worst things she did."

"Yeah, and you wanted her to make new friends, and she did," Vivi added. "Lots of people like her now."

"Including you, right?" Bailey asked.

Vivi planted her hands on her hips, making her look even more like Supergirl, the superhero she'd dressed up like. "Right."

"And including me," Tess said. She clutched her skateboard to her chest. She must have come up with a superhero who rode one, otherwise she wouldn't have been able to have it out of her locker at lunch.

"You're acting like we need your permission to be friends with somebody," Olivia told Bailey.

What Vivi and Tess had said had been bad enough. But now Olivia was turning against her too. "You don't need my permission," Bailey cried. "I don't care what you do. Go ahead, be her best friend. You practically are already."

She rushed off. If she stood there one more second, she knew she'd start crying. She wasn't going to do that. Especially not in front of her ex–best friend.

She ran into the first bathroom she came to. Luckily, it was a girls'. She could stay in there until lunch was over.

She could. But was she going to?

Bailey braced her hands on one of the sinks and stared at herself in the mirror. She'd let stupid Hannah ruin weeks and weeks of her life. Was she going to let her keep on ruining it? No. She marched towards the door.

Then paused. The knowledge that she'd have to walk into the cafeteria and see all her friends—the girls who had *been* her friends—sitting with Hannah made her feel almost dizzy, with Jell-O knees.

"If they'd rather be friends with her than me, that's fine," she whispered. "All I did was tell Hannah the truth. All I did was tell her how we all felt."

Well, how they used *to feel,* that voice in Bailey's head piped up. She ignored it. She strode down to the cafeteria, just in time to hear Principal Lopez describing that day's game, the second-to-last game of Spirit Week. "Let me remind you that the sixth grade and the eighth grade are tied," the principal told them. "A win today by one of those grades will put them into the lead."

Everybody but the seventh graders cheered. Bailey screamed her lungs out. It felt good to yell, even though she'd rather be yelling at Hannah. "But a win by the seventh grade will make them contenders for the big win!" Principal Lopez explained. The seventh graders made as much noise as they could, stamping, clapping, and shouting.

"What do you have to do to win? That's the big question," the principal continued. "Here's the answer—stand on tiptoe. Whoever stands on tiptoe the longest gets a win for their grade. So if you want to participate, get in a big circle around the outside of the room."

Bailey was in. She bet she could stand on her toes for days. Even before she'd started taking track, she had liked to run, and that meant strong calves. She took her place in the ring of contestants. When Principal Lopez gave the signal, she got up on her tiptoes. As the "Happy" song began to play, Bailey noticed that Olivia was standing almost directly across from her, all the way on the other side of the cafeteria. Hannah, Tess, and Vivi were grouped next to her.

Olivia isn't going to last long, Bailey thought with a jolt of satisfaction. *She can hardly stand on both flat feet without tripping.* Yep. Her arms were already starting to windmill. And there she went! The first one out.

The next kid didn't put his heels down until about twenty-three hippopotamuses later. Bailey had started counting by hippopotami in her head. By three hundred hippopotamuses, about two-thirds of the people were out. Bailey's legs were trembling, but only a little. She had this thing!

After another sixty hippopotamuses, there were only about ten kids left. Vivi and Tess were out, but Hannah was still in. There was no way Bailey was letting her cousin beat her.

"Okay, everyone who's left, tiptoe into the center," Principal Lopez called. Bailey minced over and found that the clear space in the middle of the room had been covered in plastic. "Make a new circle," the principal continued.

Bailey was so busy keeping on tiptoe that she hadn't realized she'd stepped into a spot next to Hannah until it was too late to move. Well, good. It would make it extrasweet when Bailey won! She glanced around and realized that she and Hannah were the only sixth graders left. That meant Bailey could win for her grade! That meant she'd be extremely valuable. And Olivia could forget about Bailey taking her to the Katy Perry contest if she was chosen MVP.

"Now we're going to make it a little more interesting," Principal Lopez told them. She signaled to Mr. Paulson and a couple of other teachers. They each walked over holding a carton of eggs. They began putting eggs under the heels of each kid still on tiptoe. That meant the next time someone went down, it would be with a *splat!* Make that a *splat, splat!*

"You stole all my friends," Bailey said under her breath, just loudly enough for Hannah to hear her over the music. "You're not going to win this too."

"I didn't steal anyone," Hannah answered, not bothering to lower her voice. Bailey was sure at least the kids closest to them had heard.

"Yeah, you did. You told them what a horrible person I was the first second you got the chance," Bailey told her, giving up on trying to speak softly.

"Well, if you weren't such a horrible person, I wouldn't have been able to tell them anything," Hannah shot back.

"Bailey! Hannah! Focus!" somebody yelled.

"You can do it, Hannah!" somebody else shouted. Bailey recognized the voice. Olivia. Cheering for Bailey's competition.

"You're the horrible person. You went tattling to my friends. And before that you went snooping in my private stuff!" Bailey cried.

Hannah jerked towards Bailey, teetered—then her feet came down. *Splat! Splat!* "That's not fair," Hannah said, raw egg spreading into little puddles around her heels. "I only wanted some paper. And Olivia *asked* me what was wrong."

"Olivia, your new best friend," Bailey snapped. "Who you stole!"

"Nobody stole me!" Olivia yelled from the sidelines. "I'm mad at you because you lied about me! I'm mad at you because of what *you* did—not because of anything Hannah did."

The words were like a slap. Bailey's knees gave way. *Splat! Splat!*

She was out too.

She'd lost the competition for her grade!

CHAPTER 17

How to Apologize

• • •

1. If you can, talk to the person face-to-face.
2. Think about what you want to say in advance.
3. Say what you did wrong.
4. Don't make excuses.
5. Say you're sorry.
6. Promise you won't do it again.
7. No matter how it goes down, don't gossip about it with other people.

Bailey stopped by the scoreboard outside the cafeteria at the end of the day. She couldn't stop herself. The seventh graders had moved into second place. Her grade was last! She felt sick inside.

But if she was honest with herself, losing the competition was only part of what was making her feel so bad, the smallest part. Olivia was furious with her; so were Tess and Vivi. Bailey wasn't sure they'd ever want to be friends with her again. And everyone in the sixth grade was mad at her for making them lose the competition.

Why had Hannah had to move here? She'd ruined everything.

"Thanks for nothing, Bailey," Taylor from her homeroom muttered as he passed by. "We could still be tied for first if you hadn't messed up."

Bailey didn't answer. He was right. She'd lost focus. She'd let herself get distracted. Olivia shouting about how mad she was at Bailey had forced all thoughts of the competition out of her head.

So shouldn't people be blaming Olivia too?

You started it. You distracted Hannah first, that little voice in the back of Bailey's head commented. She was so sick of that little voice. The most annoying thing about it? It was always right. Bailey *had* distracted Hannah. She could have waited to talk to her about what she'd done, how she'd stolen all Bailey's friends, until after the contest was over.

Bailey started the walk home, all by herself. It felt like the sidewalk had turned to quicksand. Each step took so much effort. All she wanted to do was talk to

Olivia. That's what she always did when something was bugging her. But how could she talk to Olivia about a problem that *involved* Olivia?

She half expected for her mother to start yelling at her as soon as she walked through the door. If Hannah had complained to her mother, Aunt Caitlin would have called Bailey's mom for sure. But when Bailey called out "I'm home," her mother just called a "Hi" back.

"How'd the competition go?" her mom asked, stepping into the living room.

"Okay," Bailey said. "Well, not okay really. We lost. The contest was who could stand on tiptoe the longest." She hoped she sounded normal. She didn't want a lot of questions from her mother.

"Who comes up with these crazy things?" her mom asked.

"Who knows?" Bailey said. "I guess I'll go knock out my homework." She hurried into her room and flopped down on her bed. Something was poking into her spine. She dug under her back and pulled out her spiral-bound polka-dotted notebook.

She started to throw it onto the floor, then flipped it open instead. She'd bought a new notebook especially for her first year of middle school. She'd known she'd need lots of lists. Sixth grade was an important year.

Looking at the first list made her feel a little sad. She'd made a big checkmark next to everything she'd come up with to make her first week epic. It had been great too. Now it felt like that first week was the best the year was going to be. Everything from now on was going to be awful.

She flipped the page. The next list was the one about making Hannah feel incredibly welcome. She'd been sincere when she'd written that one. And the one about making that welcome lunch perfect.

She kept flipping, pausing at the one about how to deal with Hannah annoying her, then continuing to the page with the list of how Bailey's life would be better without Hannah around. *If you'd seen a list like that about you . . .* , the insanely annoying voice in her brain began, but Bailey willed it to a stop.

The list was fair, she told herself. *Hannah practically destroyed my life.* She'd . . . She'd . . . For a second her mind went blank.

Okay, for starters, she'd tried to get into every single one of Bailey's classes—and she'd ended up in four of them. She'd bought a scarf that was almost identical to Bailey's and painted her nails like Bailey's. And she'd agreed with Bailey a bunch of times.

Was that it? There had to be more!

She'd gotten Granddad to paint Bailey's mural on *her* walls. But Bailey hadn't said that bothered her. Hannah would have picked something different if she had. Bailey had to admit that.

There had to be other things. . . .

Hannah had let herself have an allergy attack at Kitty City. That was dumb of her. She'd drunk that watermelon lemonade, even though she didn't like it. It's not as if pretending to like something you were served at someone else's house was evil. It was actually basic politeness. Ignoring one of your allergies wasn't evil either. But it was dumb. It just was.

Oh! She'd glommed on to Gus.

After Bailey had introduced them and arranged it so they'd have to spend time together.

She'd made Bailey's friends sneak around behind Bailey's back.

But they'd realized that was wrong of them, and they had apologized.

What was Bailey going to do? She'd messed everything up. Everything.

She had to start with the worst thing she'd done. She had to start with Hannah. Olivia, Tess, and Vivi had already given her the solution.

Bailey sat up and grabbed a pen from her desk. She turned to a fresh page in her notebook and began a new list: *How to Apologize*. When she finished, she sent Hannah a text.

can i come over?

The reply came back almost instantaneously.

no.

to apologize. then i'll leave.

Bailey had to count to almost two hundred hippopotamus before the answer arrived.

whatever.

That was close enough to a yes for Bailey. "Mom, I'm going to Hannah's, okay?" she called as she burst out of her room. She didn't wait for an answer. It was always okay to go over to her grandparents'. It was basically part of Bailey's own house.

When Bailey arrived, Hannah was waiting outside, the way she had so many times when Bailey showed up to walk to school with her. "I don't want my mom or our grandparents to hear," Hannah said. "That's why I'm out here. I don't want you to accuse me of tattling again."

"It's not tattling to talk to your friends," Bailey answered. This was hard. Harder even than she'd expected it to be. "And Olivia, Tess, and Vivi—they *are* your friends."

"They already admitted they met up behind your back so they could have some time without me," Hannah told her.

"I'm sorry. I'd have shriveled into a little puddle of goo if anyone had said that to me. It would have hurt so much," Bailey answered. "And anyway, now they realize you were just nervous and uncomfortable when you first started school. Once you relaxed a little and they started getting to know the real you, not the you trying to be me, they all really liked you."

Hannah crossed her arms. "But you didn't."

No lying, Bailey told herself. "No, I didn't. That wasn't because of you, though."

Hannah snorted. "Right, that's why you made that list about how to deal with how annoying I was."

"Okay, yeah, I did think you were a little annoying," Bailey admitted. "I guess you've noticed that I like to make plans."

"Yeah. Hard not to," Hannah said.

"Well, I had all these plans for my first year of middle school. And—"

"And I ruined them," Hannah interrupted.

"Not ruined. But like I thought I'd take drama this

year and I'd show the drama teacher what a great actress I was, and then maybe next year she'd give me a supporting part in one of the school plays, and then in the eighth grade I'd get the lead. So when you wanted to be my partner, it's like I couldn't do what I'd planned. No offense, but you aren't the best scene partner."

"I know. I hate that class!" Hannah burst out. "Or I did at first."

"I know! So why'd you join? Just so you'd know somebody in class?" Bailey asked. She really wanted to understand.

"Partly. But partly because I wanted you to like me," Hannah said. "That's why I did the same nails too."

"And why you choked down my watermelon lemonade?" Bailey asked.

Hannah nodded.

"I don't really choose friends based on if they like the same flavor of drink I do," Bailey said. "Or if they do their nails the same way. Olivia and I wouldn't be friends if that's how it worked. We're totally different."

Hannah sighed and sat down on the grass. Bailey sat down across from her. "It wasn't just that. My mom kept telling me how many friends you had. She was trying to make me feel better about moving here. I guess I thought if I acted like you, they'd be my friends too."

"Right now if you acted like me, you wouldn't have any friends," Bailey admitted. "Well, I still have Gus, I guess. But I won't when he finds out what I did to you." She fluffed the grass with her fingers. "I started getting really jealous of you, if you want to know the truth."

"Jealous. Of me? I don't think so," Hannah said.

"It's true. I've known Gus almost since birth. Our birthdays are two days apart. And all of a sudden he likes you more than me. He drives me crazy half the time. But when he helped you with your costume after he said he wouldn't help me, I got jealous. I was soooo jealous. Then Olivia asked you to go celebrate at Emmy's, and that's something we've always done, just the two of us. So I was even more jealous."

She glanced over her shoulder at her grandparents' house. "Also I'm jealous of you being able to be with Grandma and Granddad so much," Bailey said. She might as well get out the whole ugly truth.

"You've spent your whole life with them, though!" Hannah cried.

"I know. I'm pure evil," Bailey answered.

"Maybe not absolutely pure," Hannah said. "You did make that list about how to make me feel insanely welcome."

"And had an epic fail." She couldn't think of anything

else to say. "I'm sorry about it all." She stood up. "I could start a list on how to make it up to you, if you want."

"No more lists about me, okay?" Hannah asked. "Let's see what happens when you don't feel like you have to be nice to me."

"And when you tell me what you actually like and don't like, and what you actually want to do and not do," Bailey answered. She stood up. "I guess I should go. I have about a million more people to say I'm sorry to. I started with you because I owed you the biggest apology."

"Who else?" Hannah stood up too.

"Olivia, definitely. And Vivi and Tess. It wasn't fair to them to tell you they didn't want to be around you when I knew it wasn't true anymore."

"But you said about a million." Hannah brushed a few pieces of grass off the red-and-white-striped skirt she'd worn as part of her Captain America costume.

"Did you forget about the entire sixth grade?" Bailey asked. "We could have won today if I wasn't such a jerk."

Hannah smiled. "Yeah, I had you beat before you started fighting with me."

"That's not what I—" Bailey stopped and smiled back. "One of us would have beaten those older kids."

"If only you weren't such a jerk." Hannah's tone was teasing. "Remember the list you made about being MVP?" she asked.

"Hmm-hmm. Why?" Bailey replied.

"You had something on there about having practice sessions for the contests," Hannah said.

"But it turned out we don't find out what the challenges are in advance, so we couldn't practice," Bailey reminded her.

"I have an idea. How many kids from our class do you think you could get over here right away?" Hannah asked.

"Not as many as you could," Bailey admitted. "I'm not very popular right now."

"Okay, I'll text everyone. Here's the plan." Hannah quickly explained her idea to Bailey.

"That's awesome. That should definitely get us some bonus points!" Bailey told her. "I'll make a list of everything we're going to need. Oh, text Gus too. Ask him to bring his monster makeup."

Olivia was the first person to show up. Her face tightened when she saw Bailey. "You didn't tell me she was going to be here, Hannah."

"Can we do the short-version apology, Oh?" You

couldn't be friends with someone for more than four years without having a few fights. Once after a blowup, she and Olivia had come up with a speed apology.

"That's a best-friend thing," Olivia answered.

"I know," Bailey answered. She turned to Hannah. "You should learn it too."

"Best doesn't work that way," Hannah answered. "There can only be one best."

"I'm always telling Bailey everything doesn't fit in a list. With friends, you don't have to have a number one and a number two," Olivia said.

"And I did just promise not to make any more lists about you," Bailey told Hannah.

"Okay, so how does it work?" Hannah asked.

"Whoever is apologizing says five words that describe what they're sorry for. Then the other person says 'Accept.'"

Hannah looked from Bailey to Olivia. "What if they don't?"

"It's never happened . . . so far," Bailey said. She turned to Olivia. "Here goes. Mean. Selfish. Jealous. Jealous. Jealous."

"You said jealous three times," Olivia pointed out.

"I was very jealous," Bailey said. "Accept?"

Olivia nodded. "Accept."

Bailey turned to Hannah. "Same five. Accept?"

Hannah nodded. "Accept."

"So what did you need me for?" Gus called as he strode toward them with his box of monster makeup in one hand.

"Hannah will explain everything. I have slightly less than a million more apologies to make," Bailey answered.

CHAPTER 18

How to Have an Epic Day

· · ·

1. **Do something with your friends.**
2. **There is no #2.**

Bailey adjusted her bright green headband. It matched her leg warmers exactly. All it took to create a costume for Eighties Day was raiding her mom's closet. Her mom saved everything! She'd had enough stuff to create awesome eighties outfits for Hannah, Olivia, Tess, and Vivi.

She peeked into the main office. Ms. Durban met her gaze and gave her a fast thumbs-up. Bailey sent a text to Taylor.

go time.

Taylor lumbered around the corner, then staggered into the office wearing Bailey's dad's red letterman jacket from when he was on the basketball team in high school. Hannah grinned at Bailey, then followed Taylor, her iPhone in her hand.

Bailey waited until she saw Taylor stumble over to the counter and face-plant on top of it. Ms. Dunbar gave a loud scream. It didn't sound at all fake! Principal Lopez burst out of her office.

Time for another text. This one to Olivia and Allison. go!

Two seconds later they came lurching down the hall. As soon as they did, Bailey hit the play button on her iPod, and Michael Jackson's "Thriller" exploded out of the minispeaker.

She had already programmed the names of the second wave of dancers into her phone. She texted go! as Taylor, backed by Olivia and Allison, began jerk-walking towards the principal, Hannah filming the whole thing.

Mr. Paulson came rushing down the hall. "What's the—" he began. Then he saw the line of seven zombies, including Vivi and Tess, staggering down the hall towards him. He burst out laughing, then ran over and joined them.

Bailey hadn't been expecting that, but Mr. Paulson

rocked it. He did every claw swipe, head turn, foot stomp, and bend in sync with the other dancers. Taylor led Olivia and Allison back out of the office just in time to move into place in front of the zombies. Olivia tripped over—well, it seemed like nothing. Didn't matter. Zombies were klutzy.

Bailey texted a go! to the next wave. Principal Lopez came to the office doorway and watched as the hall filled with the dancing undead. They looked awesome, thanks to Gus's lessons in how to apply zombie makeup.

One last wave, and it was done. All the kids straightened up and walked away, heading to their lockers as if nothing unusual had happened.

"Can't have a better start to Eighties Day than a 'Thriller' flash mob," Mr. Paulson called, applauding. No one responded. They all acted like nothing out of the ordinary had happened. Bailey was so proud of them. And of Hannah for thinking up the idea and capturing it all on her phone.

"Do you think your friends could be persuaded to do a repeat performance at the three lunch periods? I can arrange late slips," Principal Lopez said.

Bailey turned to her cousin. "Hannah?"

"Absolutely," Hannah said.

A crackle of static interrupted math class a few minutes before the last bell. "It's time to announce our Spirit Week winners," Principal Lopez announced over the intercom. "The eighth graders are our champs!"

Through the walls of the classroom, Bailey could hear the cheers from the class next door, obviously a class filled with eighth graders. "And our new sixth grade class came in second." Bailey's class exploded into cheers. Hannah and Bailey gave each other a high five. "We've also tallied the votes for the MVP of each class," the principal continued.

Bailey tried to decide who she thought would win. Maybe Taylor. He'd done an awesome Michael Jackson during all three of the lunch encore performances of "Thriller." Maybe Vivi. She'd won their lunch period's game of Pictionary. She could draw anything! Maybe Daniel, who'd been Vivi's partner. Hannah definitely had a great shot. She'd been amazing at their lunch period's Name That Tune contest, plus she and Tess had gotten second in the costume contest, and everybody knew the "Thriller" flash mob was her idea.

"And now our sixth-grade MVP." Bailey realized she'd been thinking so hard she hadn't even heard who the upper-grade MVPs were. "We actually have a tie.

That's a first for us. I hope the winners will agree to share the two tickets. In no particular order, please give it up for Hannah Sullivan. And for Bailey Broadwell. Your classmates have decided you both deserve Most Valuable Player honors. All you MVPs come down to the office after class to pick up your prizes."

Bailey couldn't believe it. She'd started off the week pretty strong, earning those points for most original costume, and she'd brought those suckers in, but she'd blown the tiptoe challenge, and everybody knew it wasn't because her legs gave out. It was because she'd started a fight with her cousin.

"You realize your mouth is hanging open," Hannah said when the bell rang.

Bailey shut it. "I'm shocked," she admitted. "By me getting MVP, not you getting it," she added quickly.

"You whipped the flash mob into shape," Hannah told her. "And this morning, you were like a drill sergeant. You made sure everyone got into makeup and was in the right starting positions. You even brought a backup iPod and a backup minispeaker. I guess your lists can be a force for good."

"I hope so," Bailey answered as they headed down the hall. "So, um, can I ask you a favor?"

"I guess so." Hannah sounded a little wary.

"Olivia loves Katy Perry. If I won the tickets, I was planning to take her to make up for the not-so-great birthday day of adventure," Bailey began.

Hannah's eyebrows shot up. "And you want me to give my ticket to you, so you and Olivia can go?"

"No!" Bailey exclaimed. "No. I was just thinking . . . maybe you and Oh could go. I think you could probably manage to have fun without me. I could make you a list, if it would help."

Hannah laughed. "It would be hard. But I think we could do it." Her face got serious. "I'd feel bad if Olivia and I went without you."

"I'll make a list of ways to console myself," Bailey promised. "It's okay. Really. There's just one thing."

"What?" Hannah asked.

"You do actually like Katy Perry, don't you?" Bailey asked.

"Love, love, love her!" Hannah assured Bailey as they walked into the office. Principal Lopez was waiting for the MVPs.

"Hold it!" called a boy—Bailey thought it was Clay, photographer for the blog—as the principal handed one concert ticket to Bailey and one to Hannah. "Got to preserve the moment." *Snap!* He took their picture.

"I know you're Hannah Sullivan," he said, then

turned to Bailey. "Sorry, I don't know your name."

"I'm Hannah Sullivan's cousin," Bailey answered.

"She's Bailey Broadwell. And one of my best friends," Hannah added, throwing her arm around Bailey's shoulders.

"Nice!" Clay snapped another picture as Bailey and Hannah both gave huge smiles.